A. C. H. Smith was born in London, educated at Corpus Christi College, Cambridge and now lives in Bristol. He has worked in television, newspapers, and the theatre. His previous novels are *The Crowd* (1965), *Zero Summer* (1971) and *Treatment* (1976); he is also the author of *Orghast at Persepolis* (1972), an account of the Peter Brook/Ted Hughes theatre experiment in Persis, and *Paper Voices* (1975), a study of the popular press. He has written several plays for television, film scripts, and poetry. His other interests are cricket and racing.

Also by A. C. H. Smith

A. C. H. Smith

Edward
and Mrs Simpson

Futura Publications Limited
A Futura Book

A Futura Book

First published in Great Britain by
Weidenfeld & Nicolson in 1978

First Futura Publications edition 1978
Reprinted 1978

Edward and Mrs Simpson was written in association with
the Thames Television series produced by Andrew Brown,
scripted by Simon Raven and based on Lady Frances
Donaldson's book *Edward VIII*.

ISBN 0 7088 1313 5
Printed in Great Britain by
Hazell Watson & Viney Ltd
Aylesbury, Bucks

Futura Publications Limited
110 Warner Road
Camberwell, London SE5

CHAPTER ONE

'Atten-*shun*!'

On the order, the company of Welsh Guards moved as one man, and for a moment the noonday silence was scratched only by the faint drone of a biplane high up in the cloudless summer sky. Then there were footsteps, and occasionally a quiet word, as Prince Edward of Wales moved along the front rank of men, followed by the battalion and company officers, and His Royal Highness's Equerry, Captain Piers 'Joey' Legh.

Waiting at the end of the front rank, Sergeant Tom Boothby knew that, whatever the orders of the day said, the men were inspecting the Prince more closely than he would inspect them. The man should have been familiar enough from the newspapers, a slight figure, inches shorter than any guardsman on parade, the face normally wearing a grave expression, a wistfulness almost, emphasized by the characteristic bags under the eyes – those eyes which might twinkle into a brave, boyish grin that no one could resist. And for the soldiers there was a special bond of familiarity : this was the Prince who, ten or twelve years ago, when he was not much more than a boy, had shared the overwhelming horrors that lastingly marked the troops off from the people at home who had not been at the Battle of Passchendaele, the retreat from Caporetto, had not gazed with cynical eyes at the misery and waste, death and despair, to which so much patriotic enthusiasm had led. 'A bad shelling will always produce the Prince of Wales,' the Guards had said then, and generals and privates alike were heartened by his keen courage. He had done his duty with them, learned with them to hate war, and had thereby made himself known to the people over whom he would one day reign.

That was the man all right. But, Sergeant Boothby knew,

there was more to it. Every man in that company would be suffering awe, and pride, in the presence of royalty. Face to face with the heir to the throne, they would be inspecting him, searching out his secret, trying once again to penetrate the mystery that would anoint him king.

One thing was sure. The Prince of Wales was a different man from his father, and would prove a different king, too. Look at him up there, Sergeant Boothby was thinking, as the battalion marched past the saluting base, eyes right. The angle he wears his cap at! It's rakish, like some blooming Cossack. No one else could get away with it in the modern, disciplined British army. But on him, it was his style, his way of signalling an independence of mind that would express itself fully when he wore the crown. (Though he couldn't wear *that* at a dashing angle, could he, even him? Sergeant Boothby had to keep a straight face.) Yes, under King Edward VIII, perhaps things were going to be different. It was about time.

Piers 'Joey' Legh also had his private thoughts about the Prince's independence of mind, as he took cap, gloves and sword from him and stood in attendance, while the Prince sank into a chair in a room set aside for him in the Officers' Mess.

'Phew,' the Prince gasped, taking a cigarette from the box on the table beside him. 'Beastly hot work in this kit.' Legh moved forward with a box of matches, but the Prince had already struck one for himself. 'Don't fuss, Joey,' he told his Equerry. 'Sit down.'

'No time for that, Sir.'

The Prince puffed out a deep breath of smoke. 'What's next?' he asked, in a flat voice.

'The Sergeants' Mess.' Legh consulted his list of engagements. 'That's at twelve-twenty. Twelve-fifty, visit to the Men's Cookhouse. One-fifteen'— he paused, watching the Prince knead the corners of his eyes – 'one-fifteen, buffet lunch on the Officers' Mess lawn, with officers' wives.'

'God,' the Prince sighed, very softly, gazing over his cigarette.

6

'After lunch, watch cricket match versus the Rifle Brigade.'

'God.'

'Then attend regimental gymkhana.'

The Prince's face stirred into interest. 'There's a race, isn't there? Find out if they can mount me.'

'But Sir,' Legh answered, trying not to sound weary, 'you know your father doesn't like you steeplechasing.'

'Don't nag, Joey,' the Prince interrupted him. 'Find out if they can mount me.'

'Very well, Sir.' Legh's lips tightened.

The Prince was thinking, ironically, of all the injunctions his father had issued to him, when he was younger, on the subject of horsemanship. 'You must learn to ride and hunt properly.' That was in a letter he had received just before going up to Oxford. 'In your position it is absolutely necessary that you should ride well, as you will continually have to do so at parades, reviews, etc., and so the sooner you make up your mind to it the better. The English people like riding and it would make you very unpopular if you couldn't do so. If you can't ride, you know, I am afraid people will call you a duffer.'

Well, dammit, he had learned to ride, bravely, front-runners in point-to-points, had competed on equal terms with the best and sometimes beaten them. The politicians and the press were always nagging him to give it up, for the sake of his future, and lately his family had joined in. Now it was Legh. Well, he could have expected that. His Equerry was one of the old, aristocratic guard. Nothing he enjoyed doing could please that stuffy lot, any more than it could please his father.

'After the gymkhana,' Legh was advising him, 'there is a retreat parade. Then dinner in the Officers' Mess.'

'Not a second wasted,' the Prince remarked with an affected lightness of voice. 'Ah well, anything to please, I suppose. What time can we get away?'

'Eleven p.m. An hour after dinner ends.'

'No earlier? I mean, if dinner's once over ...'

'If you leave *immediately* after dinner it will cause offence.'

'Eleven sharp, then.' The Prince rose, crushing out his cigarette, murmuring to himself, 'And so we go on.' He stared gloomily into the cheval-glass, then switched his face to a pantomime grin. 'Smile please, Your Royal Highness,' he mocked. Taking his cap and gloves from Legh, he told him, 'One day, my face will get locked into a smile, Joey. I shall be able neither to talk nor to eat, only to smile, and smile ... But of course, that's what I'm paid for. No one would mind at all.'

'He's all smiles and charm,' the RSM was telling the Drill Sergeant, as they waited by the open door of their Mess. Behind them, two lines of sergeants waited, in a welcoming aisle, for the Prince of Wales. 'Sometimes he really means it. You can tell when he doesn't – look at his eyes, there's a kind of blank comes up behind them.'

'I do wish he'd wear his forage cap straight,' said the Drill Sergeant, who had never met the Prince. 'Bad example, you know, Sir.'

'Yes.' The RSM was thinking, as the Drill Sergeant was, of the young officers of the regiment. 'What he doesn't realize is how difficult he makes it for the likes of us, when he breaks the rules. Still, when he's sunny and really means it, you'll see, you can forgive him a crooked forage cap, you could forgive ...'

'He's coming now, Sir,' the other interrupted.

The RSM turned smartly to face inside the Mess. 'Warrant Officers and Sergeants of the Welsh Guard,' he barked, 'Atten-shun !'

Leaving his accompanying officers by the door, the Prince entered the Mess alone. While he removed his hat and gloves, handing them to the RSM, and the Drill Sergeant unbuckled his swordbelt for him, the Prince was saying, 'At ease, gentlemen, please. How are you, Regimental Sergeant Major Reeves? Still playing football for the battalion ?'

'Oh yes, Sir, thank you. But I'm getting a bit past it.'

8

'Not you,' the Prince grinned at him. He turned to the Drill Sergeant. 'You'll be Sergeant Major Owen. New here, I think?'

'Come from the Depot last month, Sir.'

'They're missing you, from what I hear.'

That's a touch of the real HRH, Sergeant Boothby was thinking. He was still to attention with the rest of the sergeants, in spite of the Prince's bidding to be at ease. How could you be at ease in his presence? He did his best to put them at ease, with remarks like that one, and no one could do better. He had been well briefed, of course, but what a memory, all the same. And yet, look at the nervous strain in Jim Owen's smile of acknowledgment. They were all of them, Prince and sergeants, on duty, and always bound to be when they met. Thank God they all knew their duty so well, and especially His Royal Highness. Without that, nothing could work, Army, country, nor Empire. That was a lesson that had been driven home a couple of years earlier, in 1926. It was the people who knew their duty, the soldiers along with thousands of ordinary middle-class people, who had kept the country's essential services running.

The Prince was moving along the ranks. 'Sergeant Evans, how are you? Sergeant Boothby, you're looking as fit as ever. Colour Sergeant James ... Aaah!' The Prince broke off, in delighted recognition of a huge pot of beer that the RSM was bearing toward him on a silver tray. He accepted it in both hands, raised it in salute to the Mess, and said, 'My compliments to all of you, gentlemen, and here's your health.' After drinking from the pot, the Prince raised it once more. 'It's good to see old friends again.'

A Welsh baritone led the singing of 'For He's a Jolly Good Fellow', which ended in loud, loyal cheers from the assembled sergeants. The smiling faces all round testified that the Prince who had charmed whole continents, on his tours abroad, had not lost his touch. There was in his manner, in his smile, something youthful, almost conspiratorial, vulnerable yet full of promise, which quickened men's hearts in a way that his father had never been able to.

*　　*　　*

At five past eleven that night, the Rolls Royce was heading back to York House, the old rambling place in St James's Palace, where as a boy the Prince had lived with his family when they were in London (and not at the dim, dank villa home in the grounds of Sandringham), and where he had chosen, after the war, to set up home for himself. Lighting a cigarette, the Prince was happier than he had been all day. Soon, he would be getting out of this mess dress and cloak, and putting on white tie and tails. He was about to resume his private life.

Next to him, in the back of the car, Legh was looking forward only to a good sleep. He had just one job left to perform, which was to nag the Prince. They both knew he was wasting his breath, but it was what he was paid for. 'I worry, Sir, we all do, lest you might be overdoing things.'

The Prince turned his face away, looking through the dark window at the suburban street lamps outside. 'We all do,' he reflected – yes, the King and Queen do, and it was them, their interests, that Legh served, not his own. But they were not all, not all that mattered to him. In his mouth he could still taste the vintage port – 1894, the year of his own birth – in which he had joined the Officers' Mess in toasting His Majesty the King, raising the glass to the portrait, which was much larger than his own portrait, next to it.

Legh was still going through the motions of advising him against a late night. 'It has been a very long day, Sir.'

'And a good one, so far,' the Prince said, 'apart from having to watch that cricket match. The race was all right, wasn't it?'

'His Majesty is not going to be pleased when he hears about it.'

'I nearly caught the bugger, didn't I? Only half a length in it, on a horse I'd never seen before. I don't call that bad.'

'You misunderstand me, Sir.'

'No I don't.' The Prince stubbed the cigarette in the ash-tray.

'His Majesty and your mother, Sir, they want you to stop racing over fences.'

'Stick to hunting, I know. But every horse I've got at Melton Mowbray is a 'chaser, Joey. It would be a shocking waste of them if all I did was hunt them a few days a year.'

'You have hurt yourself badly enough already. It caused widespread concern, Sir. You will remember that Lord Stamfordham ...'

'It wasn't that bad. And it was four years ago.'

'Nevertheless, Sir, if you would only stop it now you'd very much please the King.'

'I must have a bit of fun. I do all I can to please others in public' – Legh was nodding, he would not deny that, but the Prince did not moderate his tone – 'so I don't see why my own private life has to be rearranged to please the King.'

Legh considered relinquishing the argument, which was never going to get anywhere. The Prince had grown even more opinionated recently, probably the effect of having great responsibility, and popularity, but little power. Silence, however, would be interpreted as a pained sulking, so he answered, 'But your private life is not rearranged, Sir, is it? For instance, I don't know where you will be going on to tonight, but I respectfully doubt if it is the sort of place which ...'

'You know very well where I'm going, Joey. I'm going to the Embassy Club, and there I shall meet some friends, none of whom, I grant you, would exceptionally please the King.'

'Quite, Sir, and yet he doesn't really interfere in all that. But your riding over the sticks does concern him, because of the consequences for the future that a really serious fall could entail. So why not do just this one thing for him, Sir?'

The Prince lit another cigarette to relieve his boredom. 'What should I do for exercise?'

Legh, mistakenly thinking that his point was being accepted, grew warmer. 'You're a pretty good golfer, Sir, and golf is quite decent exercise for anybody who is, well . . .' – he saw the ditch too late and could not stop – 'getting on a bit.'

'What rubbish!' the Prince snapped. 'I'm in my thirties.'

And now there was nothing Legh could say to redeem the snub.

As the car drove into St. James's Palace, the Prince looked at his watch. 'Not bad,' he said, and beamed at Legh. 'It's all gone very smoothly. Thank you, Joey. I don't know where I'd be without you.'

* * *

It was just after one o'clock that night when the Prince entered the Embassy Club in Bond Street, and was greeted by Luigi, the *maître d'hôtel.* 'Your Royal Highness . . .'

Luigi presided over the club like a very grand regimental sergeant-major, with a dignified deference to the highest-ranked, but a tyrannical eye for anyone less. He was adored by the clientele, who told each other stories of his capricious severity. He could be forgiven his caprices, for at that period, the halfway point between two wars that ripped apart the old social fabric of Europe, it was no longer plain to see who were the commissioned officers of society and who the lower ranks. The Prince, of course, was conceded his place of honour every night he was there, which was frequently. There was not much question, either, about the dukes and earls and hereditary peers. But then there was artistic set, the writers and actors, the political crowd, MPS and press barons, the industrialists, the self-made or self-making; and the women with them, the wives, mistresses, the society hostesses and the celebrated beauties. Some of these people were rich, some famous, some powerful, some witty, or fine in looks or manners, and some were merely hoping to acquire such talents, or the reputation of having them, by association. The order of precedence could never have been agreed, even if Luigi, as he might have done, had suddenly ordained that everyone present should vote on the matter.

More important than the social order was the idea, to which everyone there could agree, that life was an entertainment. Whatever one's pursuit, the pursuit of pleasure took precedence. The ability to give pleasure, or to take it, had become the highest virtue, and was to a degree independent of the old social rankings – to a degree, but not absolutely, for the Prince pleased everyone simply by being royal.

Many of the people at the Embassy Club were privileged by having been born into wealthy families. In return, the senior generation might have expected a proper, respectful gratitude. Instead, the young people went out of their way to shock their elders, not by criticizing the source of the hereditary wealth – that would have been too much for anyone to expect – but by mocking the 'stuffy' manners and conventions that had held the upper class together. What was above all mocked was seriousness of purpose, that moral flagship of Victoria's reign. The trivial was now enshrined, flippancy was preferred to discourse, style to substance. And those who were still working their passage to privilege, the climbers and the chancers, and the *nouveaux-riches* whose injections of wealth were now increasingly needed by the fortunately born, they were delighted to ape the new etiquette. They were like the first outsiders to be admitted to a hitherto sacrosanct temple rite, careful not to make fools of themselves.

Outside the Embassy Club was a world that Darwin, Marx, and then Freud had shown to be a great machine, and it was not necessary to have read a word of their works to be imbued with the conviction that one could do precious little about anything. Flanders had proved it. Adrift from the old faiths, people were not yet anchored in the new. The war had killed off some of one's dearest friends, and with them any belief in a sacrifice for noble ideals. The

13

cynicism born of that war was nourished by its aftermath, slumps and strikes, hunger and poverty, no homes for heroes and no jobs either. Naturally, the people in the Embassy Club were not hungry (indeed, most of the *haute cuisine* they ordered was left on the plate), they had homes, plenty of them, and jobs if they chose, and they were the sons and daughters of the very men who were constantly advising the wage-earners 'not to ask too much' – but, again, it was not necessary to have suffered betrayal to be assured that life offered no safe investment for the future. All that one could do about the great machine outside was to escape it, in the company of others, for brief, amusing hours, while you may, in a place where (unlike one's home) strangers and pleasant accidents might arrive.

And what they did was what other groups under stress have done : they danced. At lunch-times and at tea-times, but most compulsively late in the evening, after the theatres and operas and formal balls had closed, the white-tie men and shingle-hair women danced together in night clubs, where they were as much at home, greeting and entertaining each other, as they were in their own drawing-rooms. The mood in the clubs was the mood of the time, for them. At the hub was the Embassy, that 'Buckingham Palace of night clubs' as it was called by the Prince himself, who was essentially a man of his generation, notwithstanding his eminent position; indeed, it was because of his position that as a young man he had felt shut off from society, the world of pleasure, which, now that it was his to enter, he embraced the more eagerly.

Tonight, as usual, there was little space left to dance in once the crush of people who had come to do it had been accommodated. Around the long, underground room, furnished luxuriously with sofas, with carnations in vases on the tablecloths, with a band on a balcony at one end, more and more chairs and tables were crammed in together, as the small hours struck, until they had so encroached on the centre that scarcely a dozen couples could find a spot to stand together and jig. The rest sat at their tables, talking, laughing, breathing in the atmosphere of rich sauces and Turkish cigarettes, ordering more drinks from the waiters, who expertly squeezed through the maze. They watched themselves and everybody else in the great gilt-framed mirrors that hung along the walls.

Over it all presided Luigi, who now led the Prince to a table at the edge of the charlestoning dance-floor. Of the four chairs around the table, one was already occupied, by Mrs Dudley Ward. She rose and bobbed a tiny curtsey, since Luigi's eye was on her. The Prince nodded in vague acknowledgment. He was more concerned about the waiters who were installing another table next to theirs.

'I don't think that we shall be needing another table,' he told Luigi.

Mrs Dudley Ward answered him. 'It's not for us, Sir. It's some Americans who have just arrived, so I told Luigi . . .'

The Prince looked at Luigi. 'Ask them to sit somewhere else, won't you?'

Mrs Dudley Ward smiled. 'There isn't anywhere else, Sir.'

The Prince was still looking at the *maître*. 'Somewhere else, Luigi.'

Luigi bowed, *molto espressivo*, his right hand over his heart. 'Your Royal Highness.' He snapped his fingers, and the table was removed.

The Prince sat down next to his old friend. She was looking at him sympathetically. 'Not very kind this evening, David?' She used the name by which he was known in his family, the last of his seven Christian names.

'I'm tired.' He did not look at her.

'Calm, calm, David.' Discreetly, below the level of the table, she placed her hand on his wrist, and stroked it soothingly with her fingertips. She spoke kindly, as though one of her children was in a temper. 'Calm, now. Bad day?'

'No,' the Prince muttered. 'Just a long one.' He gave her

a little, rueful smile, the first of the evening. 'Are the children well?'

'Yes. They send their little Prince their best love, and look forward to seeing him soon.'

'It'll have to be soon.' Now relaxing, the Prince's voice resumed his family's inflections: the vowels more closed than in Standard Oxford, the delivery more emphatic, a trace of Dickensian cockney. 'I'm off on a holiday,' he was saying, 'a sort of semi-private trip to Kenya and Uganda, then a big safari in Tanganyika.'

Mrs Dudley Ward smiled indulgently. 'Do you good. Should be fun.'

'It would be even better if you could – somehow – come.'

She was shaking her head with a regretful frown.

'Or arrange to be there when I arrive.'

'Sorry, David. We have been through this before.'

'It's always been a . . .' – he wanted a better word – 'well, dream of mine that we might be away together for a while.'

She looked at him in kindly reproof. 'It will have to remain a dream, Sir. I can't . . . And you – well, you shouldn't even ask me, you know.'

He registered the reproof with a pout. It was bad enough that he had to go on doing in public what other people expected of him, and do it with a ready smile, but that he could not have his way even in his private life was too bad. It was not as though there was any real risk of a scandal. For more than ten years he had been seeing Freda Dudley Ward almost every day, usually at five o'clock, or at least, when his public duties forbade a visit, he had telephoned her in the mornings. ('Has the baker called yet?' was her household's code name for the calls.) At the Embassy, at parties for an evening or a weekend in a country house, on the golf links or at the races, they had been seen constantly together by hundreds of people, who either knew them too little to think anything of it, or too well to say anything. Discretion was always intact. She had not needed the advice of her relative, Lord Esher, who, remembering the admirable companion of the Prince's grandfather, Edward VII, had said, 'Be like Mrs Keppel. Be discreet.' She was legally separated from her husband, an industrious Liberal MP, and had brought up her two daughters in a decidedly modern fashion, keeping them by her when guests called, where most children would have been sent upstairs. The Prince was as fond of her girls as he was utterly devoted to her.

Everybody said how good she was for him. They were so well suited. She was small, as he was, and pretty, but what was greatly attractive was her natural, unaffected charm, which did not alter whether it was the Prince she was dealing with or the paper-boy. She pursued pleasure as her friends did, but with more wisdom than most, more wry reflection, which she expressed in a high, infectiously amusing voice. A married woman was naturally not acceptable at Court as the Prince's companion, but she was as serious as anyone there about his obligations, duty and destiny. What she took less seriously was his spoilt nature. She could tease him, chaff him if he was pompous, reproach him if wayward, and he adored it. As a child, he had never had a close friend, who might have ribbed him. Nor, in his life, had he known a woman who could scold him lovingly as she did, or take him trustingly in her arms when he needed consoling.

Now, her candid eyes were telling him that she ought not to go with him to Africa. He had known that already, but still he was disappointed. He took a little sip of the champagne that Luigi had sent to his table, and lit a cigarette. The charleston had ended. He eyed the two empty chairs. 'Who's in the party?'

'Only Dickie. And Edwina.'

'Don't let them sit down. I want a few more words. Make 'em keep on dancing.'

Mrs Dudley Ward gestured to someone on the dance floor, nodded confirmation, and, as a tango struck up, turned back to the Prince. 'What is it?'

'I – I shall need someone to be with me in Africa.' He watched her face. 'Do you mind?'

She looked back at him for a while, thoughtfully, a finger on her temple. Then she gave him a small, sad smile. It had happened before, and it had never lasted, or meant anything that could wound what they had between them. Still, it always hurt a little. Instead of answering him, she observed, 'The Palace will mind.'

'The Palace minds everything. Even me and you.'

'But they tolerate it, because I'm discreet. But if the Palace see someone following you around the world . . .'

'Never mind the Palace,' he said emphatically. 'This is my own affair. Private.'

She paused again, looking levelly at him. He turned his eyes from hers, down to the table, conceding the point. After a while she asked, carefully, 'You will come back . . . after Africa?'

'Yes. I'll come back.' He looked up at her again, for a pardon.

She cocked her head to one side, and lightly asked him, 'Who are you taking?'

'I'm taking nobody. But I know of somebody who can go out, and wait for me. We can meet, as if by chance, in Nairobi.'

She teased him with her eyes. 'In my book, that adds up to, ah, Thelma Furness.' It was as though she had won a party game with her first guess, and he nodded, slightly abashed. 'She came in a moment ago,' Mrs Dudley Ward told him. 'She joined the Carisbrookes, just over there.' The Prince did not look round. 'Why don't you go and tell her that you've got my permission?'

'I'd like to dance with you first.'

'No. You dance with Lady Furness. You'll need to get in practice.' He frowned at her, and she laughed. 'Go on. By the time you've finished dancing with her, you'll find me as good as gold again.' The Prince did not move from his chair, and she changed tack. 'Some day, David, you'll have to find yourself someone who isn't married. It's not good for you, having your women already trained, so to speak. Give up your cosy matrons and strike into unmapped territory.'

She had spoken affectionately, but the Prince looked glum. 'That sounds like the Palace again.' Then his eyes, meeting hers, lit up again with the twinkle of a mischief that no one could really mind. To Mrs Dudley Ward, it was irresistible. Seeing her smile, he promised, 'I'll think about it when I get back from Africa. But the very first thing I'll do when I get back is to come and see you and the children.'

He rose. So did she, again performing the ghost of a curtsey. 'Your Royal Highness does us honour. Now go and plot with Lady Furness.'

He crossed the dance-floor and approached a table, gesturing the occupants to remain seated. He wanted no fuss now. Sitting beside Lady Furness, a more voluptuous and alluringly made-up woman than Mrs Dudley Ward, he murmured in her ear. 'Nairobi, Thelma.'

'Nairobi, Sir?' she asked, in her American accent.

'That's when you'll get your invitation to join me. On safari.'

'Safari but no farther?'

'We'll see about that. Duke won't mind your coming without him?'

'Duke, Sir, will have his own amusements.'

'Good. I like everyone to be amused.'

CHAPTER TWO

The lion was killed, and now the drums beat out a frenetic rhythm. Forty Masai tribesmen raised their spears and charged, shrieking and whooping, at the half-dozen white people seated on camp chairs, in a clearing in the bush. Scarcely six feet in front of the Prince and Lady Furness, the charge ended when the tribesmen fell to their knees with a great roar of homage, their spears brandished at arms' length above their heads. With a delighted smile, the Prince rose, stepped forward, clasped his hands around those of the kneeling chief, and raised him to his feet. The tribesmen's hearts beat with loyalty and affection, their faces beamed, the drums set up a pulse of celebration.

Arriving at Mombasa, the Prince had made a speech. The tour, he said, marked 'the completion of what I know to be the most significant chapter of my whole life hitherto. Ever since the conclusion of the Great War ten years ago, I have taken every possible opportunity of seeing for myself some unit of the Empire, until there remained only this wonderful land of promise in Eastern Africa. Today I have reached the land and the circle is complete!'

And with the beating of the Masai drums, his brief official itinerary was complete, too. As Lady Furness told him, he had certainly done his bit to hold the Empire together, smiling at 'all those ghastly government sahibs and their stringy wives and spotty daughters gawping at you like crocodiles.' Now, he was free to devote his energies to every golf course he could reach, every lion or antelope he could aim a gun at, and a select number of women who brought the safari to a halt for a day or two each. Lady Furness was not expected to mind about such detours, and Captain Legh was not permitted to mind.

What the Equerry could not tolerate was the Prince's intention to finish the last stage of the safari, forty miles through trackless bush to Voi, alone with Lady Furness in a car, while the rest struck camp. 'It's madness, Sir,' he declared, as the Prince prepared to drive off in the early morning.

'What can go wrong?' The Prince's question sounded sweet and reasonable. He was leaning on the open car, while Lady Furness waited and watched the argument. 'I know the way.'

'There *is* no way.' Legh had taken more than enough, and could barely prevent his anger and scorn from breaking through the veneer of decencies. 'There is no track from here to Voi. All you know is the direction, Sir.'

'That should suffice.'

'Until you lose it. Which can happen to anyone in the bush, even if he is a great deal more experienced than you are, Sir. Or you could have an accident. The car could break down. You could be attacked, by . . .'

'That will do, this is the unofficial part of the tour, and I have earned some rest from your ceaseless supervision.' The Prince nodded. He was opening the car door. 'Please get in, Thelma.'

'At least let me send a guide with you.' Legh said.

The Prince closed the passenger door for Lady Furness, and walked round the car, tracked by Legh. 'I have all the company I need.'

'Sir.' Legh made one last, sincere plea. 'I have a responsibility for the safety of the heir to the throne of England.'

The Prince was climbing into the driving seat. He pulled the door shut, and looked up. 'Don't be pompous, Joey,' he said, almost absent-mindedly. His pose was slightly marred when the starter required several pushes before the motor fired. Jabbing the stick into first gear, he turned to Lady Furness, and said, loudly enough for his Equerry to hear, 'Poor Joey. He's such an old woman.' He let the clutch in too quickly, and the tyres threw a cloud of dust back as the car headed off.

That afternoon, after a long picnic lunch for two, the Prince had driven only another mile when he stopped the car and leaned his head forward on the steering-wheel. 'I'm feeling rather seedy,' he muttered. Sweat was running from his forehead.

After a few minutes, he straightened up. Lady Furness saw that all the muscles of his face were taut. His shirt was dark with sweat. 'What is it?' she kept asking him. He shook his head, and drove on.

He remembered little of the drive, of how he reached Voi, was carried from the car, put onto a train and taken back to Nairobi, where he lay several days in the fever of malaria. What came first to his clearing consciousness was that Legh was saying to him, 'Now that you're on the mend, I have something rather unpleasant which I must tell you. Please read this.'

The Prince took the telegram. Looking up, he said, 'Why didn't you tell me sooner? What's to be done?'

'The light cruiser *Enterprise* is waiting at Dar-es-Salaam, Sir. From Brindisi, Signor Mussolini has offered the use of his own train, to Boulogne. Everything's packed up and ready to go the minute you're fit.'

'Well played, Joey. I *am* fit.' The Prince threw the sheets off.

Dining with the Prime Minister on the royal train from Folkestone, the Prince asked, 'Is it the opinion that – he may not recover?'

'I'm afraid I'd put it more definitely than that, Sir,' said Stanley Baldwin. 'His Majesty was sinking when I left London this afternoon.' In contrast to Legh's voice, the directness of Baldwin's was a comfort at such a time.

The Prince nodded. 'Let's hope he'll be the better for seeing me.'

'As to that, Sir – this is rather embarrassing, but the royal physicians, and your mother, did ask me to prepare you . . .'

'For what?'

'Not to see His Majesty when you reach the Palace tonight.' The Prince was taken aback, but Baldwin went on, 'Not even to go near him, was the phrase Her Majesty used.'

'Why on earth not?'

'The doctors say he must on no account be disturbed by anybody.'

The Prince looked down, frowning. He brushed a speck of ash from his trousers, and fingered the knot of his tie.

'I'm sorry to be the one to tell you this, Sir.'

The Prince nodded. 'You know, Prime Minister, I should like you to remember that you can always speak of anything to me.'

'Sir, I shall remind you of that.' In Baldwin's eye was a very grave twinkle.

'You may. As for this present matter, I think perhaps I know my father better than the doctors do.'

'Better than your mother does?'

'I understand' – the Prince chose his words – 'what is between my father and me better than my mother does.'

At Buckingham Palace, the royal physician, Lord Dawson, was firm. The King had been unconscious for a week, and his son should wait at least forty-eight hours more before going into the sick room. One never knew how much apparently unconscious people might be affected by a disturbance. When the Prince asked what was disturbing in the natural desire of a son to visit his sick father, the physician shook his head, and referred to 'differences' that he understood had taken place. Only such as took place between any father and son, the Prince replied. The physician said that he could not forbid the Prince to enter the room, but he could not take the responsibility for what might happen if he did enter.

The Prince went in. Beside the bed, he whispered, 'Father.' The King did not respond. 'Father,' more urgently.

George v half-opened one eye. 'Oh,' he growled, 'it's you, is it? Damn you, what the devil are you doing here?'

* * *

When Mrs Dudley Ward heard the story, she said it was just as Shakespeare had written it. Henry IV, on his supposed death-bed, wakes up, finds that Prince Hal has been trying on the crown, and is so angry that he recovers.

The Prince was chuckling in recognition, when she added, 'But not for very long, if I remember right. By the end of the Act . . .'

His eyes met hers, briefly, before he returned his attention to the road along which he was driving them in the green Lagonda. 'That was Henry the Fourth,' he said. 'George the Fifth will be as right as a bell, so they say, in a few days from now. God has saved the King.'

Still, the alarm had forced the Prince to reconsider his own ways. He had decided that he would give up steeplechasing, and sell all his horses. That would please his parents. Henceforth, his outdoor pursuits would be golf and gardening, to both of which he could bring all the strenuous energy of his nervous nature. That was why they were motoring around the borders of Windsor Great Park. He hoped to find a house near Sunningdale golf course, with a large garden.

In the end, they found what he wanted near Virginia Water. Fort Belvedere was an eighteenth-century royal folly on a hill, a child's idea of a castle, with battlements, towers, thirty Belgian cannons, and cannon-balls, where the sentries, Lady Diana Cooper thought, 'must be of tin'. The Prince himself called it a 'pseudo-Gothic hodgepodge'. A grace-and-favour house, it had been long neglected. The gardens and the surrounding woods promised him years of hacking, clearing, planting, and tending.

First, the interior decoration had to be done, for which Mrs Dudley Ward's help was indispensable, and Lady Furness's approval a comfort. Soon, weekend parties were being held, with tennis on the court below the battlements, swimming in the pool, and games wilder than could be played at the Embassy Club. Legh's stuffy disapproval no longer chafed the Prince. After Africa, Legh had had enough. He resigned, and was succeeded as Assistant Private Secretary by Hugh Lloyd Thomas, who was more congenial.

The Prince was happy at Fort Belvedere, when friends were there or when he was alone. Nothing gave him more pleasure than the visits of Mrs Dudley Ward with her children. He was gardening one day when Angie, fifteen years old, came running across the lawn to him, leaving her mother in the rear. 'Little Prince,' she called to him as she always did, 'little Prince.' She held her arms out as she ran.

'Hullo, Angie.' He kissed her, and offered her a rose to smell.

She smiled her sweet thanks back, and started to tug at his sleeve. 'Come on, we must go inside and put it in a vase of water.'

'Hey,' the Prince said affectionately, 'hold on. Let's wait for your mother.'

'She'll follow us. Come on.'

'No, it's rude to turn your back on people.'

'Not people you know well.'

'Yes, even then. They might be hurt.'

'Mummy's never hurt,' said Angie, arranging the world to suit herself, as a child will, without calculation. 'She's too sensible.'

'We mustn't leave anyone out, Angie. It makes them doubt whether you really love them.'

'Oh,' she said, not quite hiding her disappointment, 'you worry too much, little Prince.'

'You might think so, because you're spoiled.' He meant no unkindness, nor did she feel any, seeing the wrinkles of a smile around his eyes. The graveness behind his eyes she did not see, a gentle, grave wistfulness that her mother would have recognized at once. Mrs Dudley Ward knew about the cold emotional climate in which the Prince had been raised : the high-minded, disciplinarian father who, in his anxiety to breed a worthy heir to his throne, had seldom found a good word, or a merry one, for his children; the intensely reserved, aloof mother, who did not like the physical process of bearing children, and therefore suppressed the joy that they might have aroused in her; the disturbingly possessive nanny, the absence of any close friends, the constant weight of majesty, of duty, calling – Mrs Dudley Ward understood all of it, and so understood why it was that married women, foremost among them herself, so potently attracted the Prince. A middle-aged man, he was still trapped in his childhood, frozen in that climate, forever seeking a maternal warmth that he had been denied. She knew that wistful look all right, and recognized it now as she joined them on the lawn. 'You are so much loved, Angie,' she heard him saying. 'You've no idea of the lives some children have.'

'You mean, they're *not* loved?' Angie asked him.

'I mean that they can't be sure whether they're loved or not.' He greeted Angie's mother with a smile, but went on with what he wanted to tell the girl. 'When I was a little boy I could never be sure. There were people who seemed to love me, but I kept thinking, it might only be because I'm a prince, because one day I shall be a king.'

'But of course your mother loved you? And your father?' Angie was again rearranging the world as it should be.

'I suppose they thought they did,' the Prince replied enigmatically, and he thought of telling her how he remembered the best love, the jolliest, most uncritical affection, as that which had been given him by his grandfather, King Edward. But no – it was wrong to share one's innermost thoughts with someone so young and fresh as Angie, however fond he was of her. So he paused, and allowed Mrs Dudley Ward to turn the conversation to gardening. When the girl went into the house for orangeade, he put his arms around Freda, and kissed her with the affection of an old friend.

Any well-connected American living in London was likely to be found at cocktail time in Lady Furness's sitting-room. Apart from Thelma herself, who had married into the English nobility, there were her two sisters, who had married

American money: Gloria, a Vanderbilt by marriage, and Consuelo, who had married a Morgan, but was now Mrs Benjamin Thaw. Around these three circled the expatriate colony, and the Americans from the Embassy. In the autumn of 1930, Connie brought along a new friend, Mrs Ernest Simpson.

The Simpsons had been married for two years, and for each of them it was a second marriage. He was a reserved, scholarly man, with a gentle wit inherited from his English father, whose shipping business he now represented in London. Ernest was a man who, when the fire-alarm was raised in an hotel, emerged in the lobby several minutes after everyone else, having taken the time to put on a suit, a Guards' tie, a bowler hat, pack a neat suitcase and pick up a ready-folded umbrella.

She, a Southerner by descent and loyalty, was one of the Warfields of Baltimore, a leading business and banking firm. Although her father had died a few months after her birth, leaving her mother with very little to live on, the wealthy relations had, albeit grudgingly, provided her with the education and social schooling that her status as a Warfield demanded. She did not waste it.

Her childhood deprivations, in contrast to other girls of her class in Baltimore, forged in her a determined will to make the most of herself. If *Fannie Farmer's Cookbook* told her that asparagus was to be tied with two pieces of string, then tied with two pieces it was, not one, or three. She worked for examinations and passed them, she practised for the baseball team and was selected. With her intelligence, sharp humour, and her reputation as a 'good fellow', fun to be with, allied to a natural charm, concentrated in her dark eyes, she was always attractive to the boys she danced with, but it would have meant nothing had she not been invited to the first Bachelor's Cotillion, the coming-out ball, when she was of age. She received her invitation, and with it felt her future was assured.

Then she made an error, her first marriage, at twenty, to a naval officer. She had always said she would marry money, and the family had always said that a Warfield does not get divorced. But when Earl Winfield Spencer Jr. turned out to be so neurotically jealous that he locked her in a room for hours at a time, turned out to be an alcoholic, and obviously had no more than a humdrum career before him, she left him. She moved in the diplomatic circles of Washington, she travelled to Paris, Shanghai, Peking, but it was in New York that she met Ernest Simpson. When they married, it was in London that they set up house, at first in Upper Berkeley Street, then in Bryanston Court. They went to the theatre, ballet, opera-houses, at weekends they went sightseeing, and often they spent hours in Kensington and Chelsea seeking out antiques with which to furnish their home. They gave dinner parties, for which the steaks had been cut by the butcher according to the instructions she supplied from *Fannie Farmer's Cookbook*. Bessiewallis Warfield had learned how things should be done, and Mrs Ernest Simpson was in a position to ensure that they were done so, all the time.

And so, when she was invited by Consuelo to cocktails at Thelma's place, and found herself introduced to the Prince of Wales, she was, though nervous, determined that this, too, she would do as it should be done : that is to say, observing the proprieties, as for instance a curtsey (which she had practised for the occasion) when the Prince shook her hand, but not allowing herself to be abashed into a mere muttering of conventional phrases. Before the Prince had time to say anything after Thelma's 'Mrs Ernest Simpson', she amended it. 'Wallis Simpson, Sir.' He was not stuffy, they had told her, and he did like Americans.

'Good afternoon, Mrs Simpson,' he said. 'Wallace? A boy's name, I thought.'

She spelt it out for him. 'W-a-l-l-i-s.'

Thelma added, 'It's short for Bessiewallis, Connie said.'

Mrs Simpson looked straight at Thelma for a moment, and then smiled. 'I like to forget the Bessie.'

'Why?' the Prince asked. 'England had a good Queen Bess.'

'Bessiewallis, Sir, is a double name. Wallis from my father's side, the Warfields of Baltimore, Bessie from my mother's. Actually, from her sister.'

'But it's not because of your aunt that you would like to forget the Bessie?'

'No, Sir. I am very fond of my aunt. It is the custom of making double names that I dislike, a silly habit in America.'

'Is it?' The Prince might have mentioned that it was even more a habit in France, but he had not intended to stay long at Thelma's party, and was doing no more than he needed to be polite to a new face, albeit a not unattractive one.

'Well,' Mrs Simpson answered, 'if you don't think Bessiewallis a silly name, at least have pity on a poor friend of mine whose mother was called Rosebud, and his father Edwin. The result was Budwin.'

'Oh dear,' the Prince chuckled, shaking his head, 'Budwin, yes, I do see what you mean.' Still chuckling, he was able to nod farewell, and pass on to meet someone else.

It was six months before Mrs Simpson met the Prince again. When he said, 'I do remember Wallis, though I promise I've forgotten Bessie,' she was charmed, but not astonished. Thelma had already told her of his formidable memory. Their meeting this time was in Leicestershire, at Thelma's country house. Connie should have been there to chaperone her sister, but had been called to Paris at the last moment – would Wallis take her place? Mrs Simpson was scared of what might be expected of her socially, but Ernest persuaded her to go through with it. It was an honour, he said. Not very much was expected, in fact: some conversation at table, bridge at stakes of ten shillings a hundred. No chaperoning was required when the Prince and Thelma went off together.

After that, another six months passed, and still all Mrs Simpson knew of the Prince, apart from the gossip, was his pleasant face, impeccable manners, and what she learned from Thelma.

'Have I ever told you how I first met him?' Thelma asked, when they were drinking coffee together one afternoon in her sitting room.

'No,' Mrs Simpson said. 'Do tell.'

Thelma told. At Melton Mowbray Fair, she said, the Prince was pinning ribands on prizewinning cows, had noticed her in the crowd—

And pinned one on you? Mrs Simpson would have enjoyed saying, but it was too risky, she didn't know Thelma that well.

—and, knowing who Thelma was, the Prince had come straight over and asked her to dine with him at St James's Palace the next time she was in London.

'And we Americans have the reputation of being fast,' Mrs Simpson smiled.

Thelma had been quick to take up the invitation. 'Of course, I had to come up especially, and Duke wanted to know why, and was a bit winded when I told him.'

'What was said at dinner?'

'He asked if we could meet again.' Which they had done, and, Thelma said, using a phrase she had learned in England, 'it was a bit of a walk-over, I'm afraid. I felt, you know, so sorry for him. He's been shut out from so much.'

All the same, Mrs Simpson said, there had been at least one other source of comfort, hadn't there?

Thelma, deciding that the question sprang merely from Mrs Simpson's curiosity, took it in her stride. 'Freda Dudley Ward, you mean. She is his old flame. They met during the war, in an air-raid I believe, when he took shelter in someone's house.'

'My sister-in-law's house it was, actually.'

'Really? Well, I would call her one of his habits. One of his good habits. She's fearfully attractive and everyone adores her, and she's helping him to organize clubs for the poor and that sort of thing.'

'To help the unemployed, I believe. Feathers Clubs they're to be called. For the Prince of Wales's feathers.'

'Oh? You seem to know all about it.'

'Not really.' Mrs Simpson shrugged her shoulders with a diplomatic vagueness. 'Ernest was talking about it. He said the Prince made a speech on the subject which was recorded for broadcasting – some time this week, I think Ernest said.'

'Perhaps I'll listen. I'm not really *in* on that side of him. Freda Dudley Ward is queen there.'

'But Thelma,' Mrs Simpson told her sincerely, 'you are far more important to him.' When Thelma, in spite of herself, started to make a gesture of modest disavowal, Mrs Simpson went on, 'I've watched him with you. When you are talking to him, he wears – what shall I say? – a giving look.'

'I do have some influence,' Thelma allowed. 'For instance, I got him to have a Christmas tree at Fort Belvedere last year, for the first time. It is a royal tradition, after all.'

Mrs Simpson smiled in preparation for her next remark. 'Perhaps you could get him to have me and Ernest to Fort Belvedere, for the first time?'

'Oh, easily.'

'How kind!' Mrs Simpson let her delight register, before softening with a mild joke. 'What would it mean to be American, Thelma, if we didn't help each other in these foreign parts?'

The Prince was at Fort Belvedere, with Mrs Dudley Ward, to listen to the broadcast of his speech. He had made it in the Royal Albert Hall to an audience representing schools, universities, and the social services. 'You cannot,' he said, 'hope to influence directly the trend of international affairs, but close at hand is a domestic problem, vast and baffling if looked at in the mass, though easier to help when broken up into individual pieces. I am thinking now of each member of the unemployed population as a single, separate personality, beset by depression, labouring under a sense of frustration and futility.'

31

There were those who found a peculiar irony in the speech-writer's choice of the word 'labouring', but in general the speech aroused an immediate and overwhelming response. The call for voluntary workers to organize in order to relieve the oppressions of the poor and jobless led to the formation of more than two thousand centres. They could not alter the economic forces which created the depression, but they could ease some of the wounds, and keep alive a spirit of self-help. The Prince was known to have committed himself strenuously to his travels and speeches in the voluntary cause. Ordinary people believed that he cared about them. It augured well for the day when he would sit on the throne.

Mr and Mrs Ernest Simpson also listened to the broadcast. They felt obliged to know what had been said by the man who had just invited them to spend a weekend at Fort Belvedere.

For Mrs Simpson, the weekend was all that she had expected, and more. From the moment when they drove through the wood inside the gates, were confronted by a shadowy, fairytale mass surmounted by a softly floodlit tower, and the Prince was greeting them, overseeing the disposal of their luggage and conducting them into the house, where she noticed paintings by Canaletto, and George Stubbs, and pieces of Chippendale furniture, she was enchanted. The Prince, always an attentive host, escorted her the next afternoon around the gardens and the battlements. Thelma and Ernest caught up with them when the Prince was showing her the view of Virginia Water. Ernest had been delayed, having to fetch a sweater. He was to go labouring with the Prince and the other guests, hacking away laurel and undergrowth in the woods to make room for rhododendrons.

Apparently, the Prince must have been pleased by the weekend too, for an invitation followed: would Mr and Mrs Ernest Simpson give him the pleasure of their company at Quaglino's restaurant for a birthday party on June 19th?

'Why,' Ernest said, 'that's your birthday.'

'Yes,' Mrs Simpson replied, 'it is.'

At Quaglino's, the Prince gave her an orchid, which she potted at their flat in Bryanston Court. Soon he came to see it, as a guest to dinner.

In case Mrs Simpson did not quite understand the way things stood, Lady Furness thought she should advise her. 'Guess,' she said, 'who's at the Fort this weekend?'

'Freda Dudley Ward, of course,' Mrs Simpson answered. 'His good habit, as you put it.'

'Sometimes I'm not so sure. Consider his position.'

'A very fine position. The finest in the world perhaps. But a man must have . . . companions for his leisure. She is not only a good companion but from what you say, also an enchanting one.'

'Who has a tremendous hold over him. He is always seeing her.'

'Really?'

'But she's married and it's time Prince Charming found his own wife.'

'But Prince Charming is traditionally a bachelor.'

'He has to marry in the last act. When the time draws near for him to become king, he has to marry a girl of suitable age and rank. But our Prince shows no sign of being interested in that idea. He only likes women who are married already, like Freda Dudley Ward.'

'And Thelma Furness.'

'But don't you see, it was Freda who started it all. She got him into the habit of married women. She presented him with a ready-made family. All the comforts of marriage and none of the duties. She has made him lazy about women.'

'Why should you care about that?' Mrs Simpson asked.

'It means you're more likely to keep him. Or your share in him, that is to say.'

'Wallis, the king must have a son.'

'He's not king yet.'

'No, but King George is not getting any younger. David has to find a proper wife for the future King of England, and he must have a son – two sons, to be on the safe side, because you know King George had an elder brother who died young. And a daughter would be desirable, too. Princesses are popular, and useful for marrying to other royal families.'

'And where would that leave someone like you?'

'When he's king, and probably before that, he will have to give someone like me up. And someone like Freda Dudley Ward.'

'You have been exceptionally English in some respects, Thelma. If I were you, I should never bow myself out so tactfully. I remain, at heart, American.'

'Yes. I don't think you understand. When he finds a suitable wife, it would be out of the question for me or anyone to stand in his way, or to make even the slightest awkwardness. It is not as though I could marry him myself.'

'Why not?' Mrs Simpson asked, lightly, but not frivolously. 'You could always get a divorce from Duke, on his record.'

'Wallis Simpson.' Thelma shook her head, slightly baffled. 'Future Kings of England do not marry divorced women. Surely you . . .'

'They never have done yet, you mean,' Mrs Simpson interrupted.

Thelma saw the funny side, and laughed. She stood looking out of the window. 'Oh my, you still have plenty to learn about the English, Wallis.'

It was early in 1934 when Thelma Furness left on a visit to America. The day before she sailed, she invited Mrs Simpson for a cocktail, and told her, 'He said he's going to miss me very much.'

'Oh, Thelma, the little man is going to be so lonely.'

34

'Yes ... but distance makes the heart grow fonder, and he'll be busy with tours these next few weeks including a real horror in Wales. So he won't have much time to be feeling sorry for himself. But you look after him for me when he's in London, Wallis. See he doesn't get into any mischief.'

Mrs Simpson smiled, and patted Lady Furness's hand. 'If I see him at all, I'll do my best.'

Mrs Simpson had formed the habit of having a few friends round for drinks early in the evening. She was elated when the Prince now became a frequent caller at such times. If he outstayed the other guests, he was invited to take pot-luck at the dinner-table. That happened several times, always on evenings when Ernest Simpson chanced to have brought papers home with him to work on in his study. After a while, Ernest habitually left them alone in the sitting room, whether or not he had papers to attend to.

'The usual?' Mrs Simpson asked the Prince one evening.

'Please.'

She poured a Vichy water for him, and a small Benedictine for herself. 'Thelma is having a busy time in America, I hear.'

'Ah. She sends wires, but they don't tell me much about what she's up to.'

'She's such a scatty creature, I don't suppose she is too sure herself about what she's up to.'

Mrs Dudley Ward was carefully arranging some flowers in a vase beside her elder daughter's empty bed. Angie added a jug of lemonade and a box of chocolates, the least she could do to raise her sister's spirits. Her elder sister was soon to return home from the hospital bed where she had been lying for weeks, after an operation for appendicitis which led to complications, and the worst of it was that her little Prince had not been to see her. She had continually fingered the gold bracelet she always wore, which he had given her on the occasion of her being presented as

35

a débutante at Court before Their Majesties. She thought about all the lovely weekends at Fort Belvedere, the gardening, and walking in the woods, and playing Minoru in the evenings by the fire. Why, she had asked her sister Angie, had he not visited her during this boring convalescence? Their mother kept saying that he was very busy just now. But he had always been very busy. That was what being the Prince of Wales meant. Never so busy, however, that he hadn't any time for them. Until now.

'Yes. I think they'll do,' Mrs Dudley Ward said, standing back from the flowers.

'They're lovely, Mummy,' Angie said admiringly, as she sat down on the bed to leaf through some magazines she had collected for her sister's benefit. 'I say, Mummy, listen to this,' she cried, noticing an interesting headline, 'it's about that beastly Lady Furness.'

'She is, in fact, rather a charming woman, Angie,' Freda Dudley Ward gently rebuked her daughter.

'Well, it says here she had dinner five times with Aly Khan on her way back from America. Is that charming, Mummy?'

'Don't be so judging.'

'The paper says he cancelled several important engagements so as to get on the same boat as her. Do you think the little Prince will be cross with Lady Furness?'

Her mother glanced at the paper. 'It wouldn't surprise me.'

'Good,' Angie declared, 'Now he'll spend more of his time with us.'

'But haven't you noticed anything?'

'What do you mean?'

'I didn't think about it at all during the illness, but it's more than three weeks since he telephoned.'

'That's not like him. Ring and see what's the matter.'

Mrs Dudley Ward telephoned St James's Palace later in the day. After a wait, she was told by the telephonist that the Prince was not free to speak to her, but would she leave a message?

36

'Please tell him, Martha, that I rang up to say that my daughter is mending very fast, and the doctor says that it will be perfectly all right for her to have visitors now. She will be home today and she would be grateful if he could come.'

She hung up, reflecting. Never in seventeen years had so long a time gone by without the sound of his voice.

'Darling,' Mrs Simpson said when the maid showed Lady Furness into the boudoir at Bryanston Court, 'how marvellous to see you again.' They gave each other a kiss on the cheek. 'But Thelma, you don't look very well.'

'I've brought a cold back with me. At least it's one thing I didn't have to pay duty on. But that's not it, Wallis.' She was frowning, her eyes candidly appealing to Mrs Simpson for some sort of help.

Mrs Simpson dismissed the maid. 'We don't want to be disturbed for any reason. If anyone rings, answer it and say I'm out.'

'Wallis,' Thelma said when they were alone, 'the Prince looked in at lunchtime, and he was very peculiar. Can you tell me anything?'

'How do you mean, peculiar?'

'He seems to have heard some story about Aly Khan.' Thelma might have added that the Prince had hardly pecked her cheek in welcome, stayed only five minutes, and left with the remark, 'After such lavish entertainments at sea, I hope you will not disdain what is on offer at the Fort, if you would like to come down for the weekend.'

'Newspaper garbage,' Mrs Simpson was reassuring her. 'We none of us paid any attention to it. Darling, I assure you that the little man was just lost without you. Just lost.'

Thelma's frown had not lifted. 'So nothing's changed?' she asked doubtfully.

The maid returned, and told Mrs Simpson, 'Excuse me, ma'am. Telephone.'

'I told you to say I was out.'

The maid was embarrassed. 'It's His Royal Highness, ma'am.'

Mrs Simpson rose. She left the room without looking at Thelma. The maid, following, closed the door behind them. Thelma was not too proud to go to the door and listen to what she could catch of the telephone conversation. 'Yes,' she heard Mrs Simpson say, 'Yes, I think so ... Thelma is here now ... Of course, quite ... Yes, I do understand, Sir. Goodbye.' Thelma swiftly regained her chair.

As Mrs Simpson re-entered, and sat down, Thelma looked hard at her. 'Wallis?' she asked, slowly.

'Yes, Thelma?'

Thelma was on the edge of her seat. Now, after a pause, she sat back, and took a deep breath. 'Wallis,' she said, in nearly a monotone, 'the Prince has asked me to the Fort for the weekend. Would you and Ernest care to come down too? It might help.'

'Of course.' Mrs Simpson accepted without needing a moment for reflection. 'Of course we'll be there, darling. You can count on us,' she added figuratively.

When Lady Furness arrived at Fort Belvedere that Friday, she found Mrs Simpson there already, having tea with the Prince.

'Thelma,' the Prince said, rising, 'I'm sorry I wasn't there to meet you when you arrived just now.'

Mrs Simpson, smiling in sweet welcome, explained, 'We were in the garden.'

The Prince nodded. 'Come and sit down, Thelma.'

Mrs Simpson, sitting with the teapot beside her in the position of 'mother', was saying, 'His Royal Highness wouldn't change his shoes and socks when he came in, although it was wet outside. I warned him he might catch cold.'

'There's a lot of it about,' Lady Furness remarked in a flat voice.

'Let me pour you a cup of tea,' Mrs Simpson offered. 'With milk only, I know.'

'Is Ernest here?' Lady Furness asked.

'He's upstairs, having a rest.' As she passed the cup to Lady Furness, Mrs Simpson asked the Prince, 'And you, Sir? Another cup of your lovely English tea? With milk, but I'll not give you any sugar, because it's bad for you.' Her eyes caught those of Lady Furness, who by now was shaking her head to warn her friend that one did not speak like that to the Prince. Mrs Simpson took no notice of the warning. Instead, seeing the Prince reach for the sugar-bowl, she lightly slapped his hand away. 'No.' She grinned. 'Naughty.'

Lady Furness sat quite still, in appalled silence. The cup trembled a little in her hand, making rings on the surface of the tea. Even at forty, the Prince's looks were often described in the newspapers as 'boyish'. But to hear him called 'naughty', to his face . . .

Mrs Simpson's eyes met hers again. Then she put out her hand and took the Prince's, just under the wrist, while she went on looking straight at Lady Furness, boldly and defiantly. The Prince, who had been staring down at his lap, now raised his eyes too, and looked coolly at Lady Furness. It was almost as though they were posing for a portrait, an informal study of a domestic scene.

Lady Furness could stand it no longer. She put down her cup, rose, left the room, quickly, and motored back to London. Her luggage had to be sent on to her.

Mrs Dudley Ward was on the telephone to St James's Palace again. Her voice was urgent. 'Martha, can I speak to HRH, please? I do know he's got a lot on, but I have been expecting to hear from him. He did get my message the other day about Pempie?'

The voice of the telephonist, after years of putting Mrs Dudley Ward and the Prince through to each other, was the voice of a friend: a friend, now, in great distress. 'I have something so terrible to tell you that I don't know how to say it.'

'Just tell me what the matter is, Martha, dear.'

'I have orders not to put you through.'

'Thank you, Martha. Goodbye.'

As she hung up, a tear shone in Mrs Dudley Ward's eye. She had a presentiment that she would never meet the Prince again.

She entered the bedroom, and, before her daughter could speak, said, 'No, darling, I have not spoken to the Prince.' She sat down on the bed, unable to hide her shock. 'It seems he does not wish to speak with me.'

The girl stared, then put out her hand, took her mother's, and held it tightly.

CHAPTER THREE

At a period when wars and revolutions were knocking down the monarchies of Europe like so many playing-card castles, the British crown still commanded the reverent esteem and popular enthusiasm that Queen Victoria had engendered. The Silver Jubilee of George V and Queen Mary would be an emotional climax of patriotism.

Not only as heir to that crown but more especially for his own sake, the Prince enjoyed an unparalleled popularity. Through his world-wide travels, and the reports and pictures of him, that modern communications made possible, millions were captive to his charm, energy, fetching appearance, his great ability to please, and his expressed concern for the dispossessed and downtrodden. The private petulance, stubbornly held opinions, moodiness, unpunctuality, were largely unseen, thanks to the veils of discretion which also concealed his social life and affairs. He was, moreover, recognized as a man particularly of his generation, the generation who had left their illusions in the mud of Flanders, but had also left behind the stuffy protocol and old-fashioned prejudices of their parents. He saw himself as a representative of the young, and that is how he was seen by others. As king, it was expected that he would democratize the monarchy. He expected it himself. He was already at one with the hopes of the people over whom he would reign. If sometimes he was chafed by his present and future obligations, his reluctance was always set aside by his sense of duty. It was instinct in him. It had been bred into the bone.

The family régime that had bred that into him had, however, also instilled in him the pathetic weakness he had for married women, the sort of woman who, as he had hinted to Angie, would supply him with the mothering love, the care for him as a person, that the disciplines of his father and mother had abnormally lacked. What Mrs Simpson had now brought him, more plentifully than any of her predecessors, was a comfort so ardently needed that his gratitude and love for her overwhelmed every other consideration in his private life : as it had swiftly swept aside any affectionate tact he might have had in concluding his friendships with Mrs Dudley Ward and Lady Furness. Nothing else, no one else, mattered in comparison with Wallis. His slavish devotion to her aroused more gossip and scandal, in their social circle, within a few weeks of their now definite attachment than the Prince had stirred up in the whole of his forty years. There was, too a sense of excitement, of opportunity. When the Prince's favourite changes, old advantages of connection are cancelled, and new connections see their chance of dancing into the limelight. The Prince did nothing to deter such hopes. He was too elated to care.

The parties at Fort Belvedere now became more glittering and busy than before, attended by numbers of people anxious to make the acquaintance of Mrs Simpson – 'and Mr Simpson' they added, for the sake of appearances. She was just as anxious to be met by them. Throughout the evening, it was clear who was the hostess in that bachelor household. She whispered and nudged the Prince into doing what she saw needed to be done, a greeting here, a conversation there, someone leaving who wanted to say goodbye. She deftly directed the waiters, and could summon the butler with an eye. Her engaging drawl charmed any guest when she wished. It was all noticed.

'Not leaving us, Chips?'

'With His Royal Highness's kind permission' – Henry Channon had collected enough gossip for one day. 'Yes, I have a 'plane to catch early in the morning.'

'A Sunday 'plane?' Mrs Simpson asked. 'Business or pleasure?'

'Neither,' Channon answered, 'Just family.'

'Money talk?' asked Mrs Simpson, half turning so that she could look across the room for the Prince. She saw him coming toward her, accompanied by Lady Diana Cooper. The Prince, as was now his habit at weekends, was wearing a kilt (at which sensitive guests winced, as it implied that the Prince intended to finish the party by serenading them on his bagpipes). Before Mrs Simpson turned back to Channon, she noticed her husband on the far side of the room, eating a canapé, alone.

'Money talk, of course,' Channon was saying. 'What else could any family have to discuss?' Not wishing to enter a fresh converastion, with the Prince and Lady Diana, he put out his hand in farewell, and accidentally knocked Mrs Simpson's evening bag from her wrist as she turned back to him. 'I'm so sorry,' he apologized, and bent down to retrieve it.

'That's quite all right, Chips,' she said, as he handed the bag back to her, adding, for the amusement of the Prince and Lady Diana as they joined her, 'I like to see the English grovelling before me.'

'You're forgetting, my dear,' Lady Diana said, 'Mr Channon, like you, is transatlantic.'

The shadow of annoyance that passed across Mrs Simpson's face was observed by several of the guests. Anything that Mrs Simpson did at such gatherings was observed, and made the subject of comment and speculation at the side of the room.

Lord Beaverbrook, after meeting her, said that he found her as simple in character, and as inexperienced in worldly affairs, as she declared she was, but that she had sound common sense. She was not attractive, but pleasing. He was particularly struck by the assurance with which she received kisses of greeting from the female guests at Fort Belvedere, but never returned them. 'Chips' Channon also remarked in his diary on her confident manners. Lady Furness had reason to agree that Mrs Simpson was not beautiful, 'in fact not even pretty', but conceded that her successful rival had a distinct charm and a sense of humour. Her eloquent eyes were her best feature – though Cecil Beaton found them 'slightly froglike' – her large hands her worst. No one doubted her intelligence, though some thought it a wise kind of intelligence, others just cleverness. She was, it was said, 'never embarrassed, never ill at ease'. To people who did not experience her charm, or resisted it, she could seem 'unprepossessing'. Others found her frankness and gaiety, and calm dignity, magnetic. All in all, she combined brain and charm as effectively in London, at the age of thirty-eight, as she had twenty years earlier, at Bachelors' Cotillion.

Something else would have been recognized in Baltimore, her determination. The observers at the side of the room agreed that she exercised a 'complete power over the Prince of Wales', an 'extraordinary hold'. She organized his appearance, his social behaviour, his tastes and his habits.

Some things she could not change. Her attempts to engage him in the literary, cultured drawing-rooms of the West End were doomed by his upbringing, when his parents had shielded him from contact with any cultivated mind, any advanced thinking, anyone who could be called an intellectual or an artist. He would suffer himself to be installed in a box at the opera or the ballet, until the interval at least, but his favourite entertainment was the cinema, where he could sit in the darkness with his head on her shoulder, giggling from time to time.

She had some difficulty, too, in persuading him to moderate his taste in clothes, when he was off duty. He had been passionately interested in what he wore ever since his first opportunity to choose for himself, at Oxford. He liked bright colours and large patterns, loud checks, informal sports-jackets, plus-fours, or the new fashion for turn-ups. His clothes were thought vulgar by some people, among them the King, which was of course a motive for the Prince's persistence in wearing them. The King was also deeply interested in clothes, believing, from his conservative point of view, that one could infallibly judge a man's morals by them, spot a cad or a bounder from one glance at the cut of his suit. It was, indeed, a family characteristic : the Prince's grandfather had been unable to enjoy an evening if one of the guests was wearing the wrong tie. Mrs Simpson managed to banish the most outlandish garments from the Prince's wardrobe, but she realized that to reform his tastes completely she would have to settle in for a long campaign of attrition.

For the present, with her astute tactical sense, she attended to what she could realistically hope to change. She was firm about his smoking habits, forbidding him to light a cigarette or cigar in formal surroundings, at the theatre, for instance, or when guests were still arriving at a party. She used her influence to persuade him to be polite and friendly to people of importance, and to mend his bad habit of unpunctuality. She was the first to praise him when he went out of his way to please people, even to the extent of leading the applause when he marched into the drawing room at the Fort blowing his bagpipes. She approved when the Prince, who enjoyed domestic life, mixed and poured the cocktails himself, or restlessly jumped up to fetch the soda-water or the potatoes for his guests at dinner. She liked to say that she always had taken a special interest in his public work, and he did not deny it, forgetting, or choosing to forget, that Mrs Dudley Ward was even more busily active, as she would be for years afterwards, in funding and running the Feathers Club, named for him.

Slowly, but unremittingly, in that summer of 1934, Mrs Simpson established herself as the first lady of Fort Belvedere, arranging the furniture, overseeing the running of the house, selecting the meals as Fannie Farmer would. The domestic staff resented it all, but had no right of appeal.

The weekend house-parties usually spent their afternoons by the swimming-pool, after a morning when the men attacked the undergrowth in the woods. There were long chairs and mattresses to recline on, and dumb-waiters bearing cigarettes and drinks. Sometimes they had lunch by the pool. The Prince had never eaten much more than an apple at midday, and saw no reason to lay on large meals for anyone else.

Ernest Simpson was still customarily invited with his wife, but was increasingly an isolated, plump figure. 'He always seems rather out of things,' the Prince remarked to Mrs Simpson. 'Would he like to be introduced to someone new, do you think?'

'He's already been introduced to everyone here.' She shook her head. 'He has so little leisure that he's too worn out to enjoy what he does get.'

'What should I do about him, do you suppose?'

Mrs Simpson gave the Prince a curious look.

'Anything to please,' he explained, 'anything to please.'

She thought. 'It's difficult to say. Best to leave him be, I think. The problem's quite near solving itself. He has so much work on hand, you see, that he will be unable to take any more time away from London, even at weekends, for the next month at least.'

'That's a bit stiff.' The Prince was sympathetic. 'Can't we do anything to make it up to him?'

'He feels that the work itself is recompense enough. That is all he really lives for.'

'All work and no play makes Jack a dull boy.'

Mrs Simpson's eye met the Prince's. 'I couldn't agree more.'

The Prince looked up. 'Lunch,' he said, seeing the butler, Osborn, leading a line of servants with covered trays.

'Ah.' Mrs Simpson stood up. 'I hope they will be serving the club sandwiches I suggested.'

'Club sandwiches?'

'An American speciality. Toasted, two layers, chicken, lettuce, mayonnaise, bacon and egg.'

'Sounds delicious.' The Prince followed her towards the buffet table.

As Mrs Simpson had suspected, from the stuffy manner of the Head Chef on receiving the suggestion, there were no club sandwiches. She expressed her disappointment to the guests crowding around the table. The Prince at once took the matter up with Osborn. 'Where are the club sandwiches Mrs Simpson asked for?'

She corrected him gently. 'Suggested, Sir.'

'If Mrs Simpson makes a suggestion, you comply with it.'

The butler said, 'The suggestion was not conveyed to me, Your Royal Highness.'

'I'm not blaming you. But just send to tell the Head Chef to prepare club sandwiches now for all my guests.'

Mrs Simpson intervened. 'Oh, not now, Sir. There will be plenty more opportunities for club sandwiches.'

'Yes, there will be.' The Prince turned to Osborn again. 'Kindly tell the Head Chef, the next time we have lunch out here, there will be club sandwiches.'

Mrs Simpson was in her sitting-room at Bryanston Court, reading Michael Arlen's *Piracy*, when her husband bustled in with a brief-case and hat, on his way to the study. 'Ernest, I must talk with you.'

Simpson, who was so perfectly aware of the position they had reached that he had no illusions about why he was working so hard, stopped in mid-bustle, still clutching his brief-case. 'I have a lot of urgent papers in here, Wallis.'

'You must talk to me first.'

He smiled, very sweetly. 'You mean, I must listen to you first.'

'Ernest, for August the Prince has taken a house in Biarritz.'

Simpson nodded. In his unhappiness, his mind was continually throwing up quirky thoughts, and now he considered replying: I knew it would end up at the Ritz. He suppressed his smile, as he had been suppressing it for several months, allowing just a twinkle to show through, suggestive of an inner spirit that his wife could not humiliate. 'Biarritz,' he simply repeated, in a carefully neutral voice.

'We are invited to stay with him. This is an opportunity not to be missed.'

That was rich. Still courteous, Simpson nodded again. 'As you well know, Wallis, I have already engaged myself

47

irrevocably to go to America in August, on business. It is, strictly speaking, your business to accompany me. However, we should not speak strictly, should we? If you wish, you should go to Biarritz.'

'Thank you, Ernest.'

'I am not a difficult man to deal with, nor, I hope, shall I become one. But there is one matter to be settled. You must be escorted.'

She frowned, puzzled.

'Chaperoned,' he said.

'But I will not be unaccompanied with him. There will be other guests, and members of his household.'

'You should have someone in your corner of the ring, if I may put it so. I am sure the Prince would agree with me.'

Mrs Simpson took the point, and after giving it some thought said, 'I think I may have the answer – dear Aunt Bessie Merryman.' While Simpson considered, she added, 'A model of propriety,' remembering how her mother's sister had objected to the first divorce.

'Yes,' Simpson allowed, 'I dare say your Aunt Bessie will do very well as your second. Her advice between the rounds will be sound, if you choose to heed it.'

Aunt Bessie Merryman had once before played a vital part in securing her niece's happiness, when she had rescued the five-year-old Wallis and her mother from the lonely, dreary life they were leading in a cheap hotel in Baltimore, and taking them into her own home. But that was a lifetime ago, and nowadays Aunt Bessie was a formidable matron, built like a bell.

She sat squarely in the house at Biarritz, examining a piece of tatting stretched on a frame. The evening light through the french windows danced on the wall, reflected from the waves only a pebble's-throw from the house.

Hugh Lloyd Thomas, the amenable successor to Legh, came in wearing a white tuxedo. 'Good evening, Mrs

Merryman. We are early for dinner. His Royal Highness won't be joining us for a quarter of an hour at least.'

'He won't be joining us at all.' Aunt Bessie pointed to the tatting. 'What's this?'

'Needlework. Excuse me, what did you say about . . .'

'I can see it's needlework. Whose needlework is it? It ain't mine. It don't belong to the little wife of that Commander . . .'

'Buist. Did you say . . .'

'She ain't the type. And it sure ain't Wallis's. So whose is it?'

'HRH's. I'm sorry, but did . . .'

'That' – she silenced him – 'is the *Prince's*?'

'He likes to do a little tatting. He says it's more useful than detective stories as a relaxation.'

'I hope it worked. Because they've gone out.'

'HRH and . . .' Lloyd Thomas smoothed the strands of hair across his bald head.

'And my niece. They're having dinner along the coast somewhere. Without benefit of chaperone, as you can see.'

'I always gathered that the appointment was, ah, a titular one.'

'Oh, I shan't be putting my nose in where it's not wanted. But I do think, Mr Thomas . . .'

'Lloyd Thomas.'

'. . . the chaperone ought to be seen with them in public. It's the look of the thing.'

Lloyd Thomas smiled wryly. 'HRH has never been much concerned with the look of the thing.'

'But the thing itself is still respectable. So why shouldn't it *look* respectable?'

'I imagine that he simply wants to be alone with her. Privacy is a rare treat for a member of the royal family, so is he to be much blamed for stealing a little?'

Privacy was not so easily stolen. Whether it was the waiter who bowed every time he served them, or one of the other diners, who had made the identification, every pair of eyes in the Basque bistro stalked the royal table, and every tongue was murmuring discreetly.

The Prince was soothing Mrs Simpson's doubts about the propriety of having slipped out together. 'Now it's happened once, they'll accept it, since there is a precedent of some sort, and next time we need not be quite so furtive. They'll not complain provided we don't overdo it.'

'Suppose they did complain?'

'That would be a pity. I like to keep everyone happy, and they won't be happy unless they stop complaining.' He smiled, to take away the acid in the remark. Seeing her face still unreassured, he gave her the surprise he had been saving. 'Anyway, at the end of this fortnight, there can't be any more such problems.'

'Why?' His finality made her nervous.

'We shall all be off on the *Rosaura*.'

'The . . .?'

'Lord Moyne's yacht. A little cruise. Would you enjoy that, Wallis?' On a boat, he was thinking, we might even get some privacy.

The look in her eyes answered him.

It would have tempered her enthusiasm if she had been at Sandringham and seen George V and Queen Mary receive the news that the entire Biarritz party was sailing on to Cannes.

> *Tea for two*
> *And two for tea*
> *And me for you*
> *And you for me . . .*

Through the huge horn of the gramophone, the song filled the lounge of the *Rosaura*, where only three couples were dancing. Among those sitting at tables was Aunt Bessie, with a highball. She did not even move her eyes to watch when one of the couples danced straight out of the door, into the night air.

Very faint on the port horizon were the lights of Barce-

Iona, outshone by the intensity of the stars. As the lounge door swung to, and the Prince and Mrs Simpson walked hand in hand along the deck, the song faded behind them, under the sounds of the sea, and the night breeze, and the pulse of the engine. They came to a gangway leading down. A sign warned: DANGER – PLEASE DO NOT GO BEYOND THIS POINT.

'What's down there?' Mrs Simpson wanted to know.

'Anchors, cables, capstans,' the Prince answered.

'Of course, you were bred to the sea.'

'Trained to it.'

'All right, trained.'

'There are a number of things I have been trained to about which I know quite astonishingly little, nor am I curious to learn any more.' He stood indecisively holding her hand. 'Would you like to sit down?' He indicated a pair of reclining deck-chairs, under a canopy.

She shivered, and let go of his hand.

'Shall we get you a wrap from your cabin?'

'I'm not cold.'

'You shivered.'

'That was something else.' She paused. 'I must go to my cabin.'

He perched on one of the chairs, and looked up at her. Although she could not see his face clearly, she knew the appealing, wistful look it wore, as he asked, 'Shall you be coming out again, later on?'

'Not tonight, Sir.' She kept her voice cool. '*Hasta mañana*, as I believe they say in these parts.' She curtsied lightly, ironically, but slowly enough to leave some meaning in the action.

When she had left, the Prince sat down full length in the chair, and smoked several cigarettes before retiring to his cabin.

In the hot Mediterranean sunshine the next day, the Prince was sunbathing on deck, wearing only a pair of baggy, checked shorts. In the deck-chair next to him was Mrs Simpson, in a bathing costume.

Hugh Lloyd Thomas, dressed in a summer suit, with tie, crossed the deck to tell the Prince, 'We're coming in to Toulon, Sir. I expect you'd like to change.'

'Change?'

'Into some clothes, Sir. There may be compliments.'

'But I'm on holiday. Why can't I dress like any other human being in a hot climate?'

'Sir, it is known that you are sailing on the *Rosaura*, and there could well be compliments. Your Royal Highness will not need to be reminded how readily the French take offence. Eagerly, one might say, Sir.'

'Fend them off if you can, Hugh. If not, well, anything to cement the *entente cordiale*.'

'*Noblesse oblige*,' Mrs Simpson murmured.

'But' – the Prince switched to a Scottish accent, and thumped his bare chest heartily – 'a Prince is a man for a' that, and there's nothing offensive about seeing him bare buff.'

'No, Sir,' Lloyd Thomas said, 'but it is possible that the informality, the casualness, may be resented.'

'Look at my informality, Wallis.' The Prince stroked his arms and sides. 'Survey my casualness.' He patted his belly. 'Could they possibly be resented, even in France?'

'No, Sir.' Mrs Simpson smiled. 'They are far too pretty, even if slightly overcooked.'

The Prince grinned up at Lloyd Thomas, and nodded, as if to say, there you are. The Assistant Private Secretary went off with a mildly disappointed air.

> *You say tomatoes*
> *And I say tomatoes*
> *You say potatoes*
> *And I say potatoes…*

'Wallis,' the Prince whispered in her ear, as they danced again in the lounge that evening, 'tell me a secret?'

She squeezed his hand. 'Yes?'

'It's a delicate matter.'

'Go on.'

'Is it really true that anyone in America actually does say po-tah-toes?'

'I'll tell you another secret,' she whispered, her eyes laughing. 'Do you know what the French call tomatoes?'

'Tell me.'

'*Pommes d'amour.*'

'I think, don't you, it's time to take the air.'

Strolling along the deck, he asked, 'Well, was I good to-day?'

She squeezed his hand again. 'You didn't please poor HLT, but even with him you were sunny tempered. And with everybody else.'

'Hugh Lloyd Thomas ...' The Prince shook his head, and mimicked, 'Into some clothes, Sir.' He sighed. 'It's enough to make a man rip them all off. Now I come to think of it, all my life I've been yearning to rip all my clothes off.'

She laughed, laughed so much that she had to stand back from him, fingers interlaced, laughing at the sea.

'What's so funny?' He was a little perplexed.

When she could, she answered. 'The idea, the idea of your *ripping* everything off, in front of HLT, and that little Mayor of Toulon ... So absurd, you are. So extreme.'

'That is the man rebelling against the Prince.'

She stopped laughing, and when she spoke it was in a low, intense voice. 'The man *is* the Prince. You cannot separate them. Nor can I. My Prince.'

'What sort of woman can she be to lead him a dance like this?' the King expostulated, when news reached Sandringham that the Prince had again extended his holiday, and from Cannes was sailing on to Genoa, and then motoring to Lake Como. The King stared gloomily through the window of the Rolls Royce. On the heath, a party of men were advancing in line, rough shooting. 'He should have been here,' the King said, 'helping me look after my guests.

He knows I'm not up to it any more. With this damned stick.' He banged the walking-stick angrily on the floor of the car. Queen Mary, next to him on the rear seat, nodded in sympathy. The King went on, 'He knows one of us ought to be out there making sure everything's being properly done, not just sitting on his arse in a car and watching.'

'He never said he would come here this year,' the Queen remarked, more as a point of information than in defence of her son.

The King peered anxiously through the window again, breathing hard, muttering, 'Pray God there are enough birds.' At length, he allowed the point. 'No, he never said that he would come here. But he did have other engagements, firm ones, all of which he has broken just in order to prolong this – this carnival progress across Europe.'

'They were only minor engagements.'

The King barked in instant reproof, 'Engagements to relatively small people.'

Mary bowed her head slightly, acknowledging her brief moral lapse.

'To small people,' the King went on, 'and therefore engagements carrying the greatest obligation of all. As my son, he must surely know that.' He glared through the window again. 'God send enough birds for good sport.' Addressing himself as much to God as to Mary, he repeated, 'What sort of woman can she be?'

'David, you must not overdo it,' Wallis whispered to the Prince. 'Everything may be taken from us if we are too greedy too quickly.'

She had seen him wheedle Lloyd Thomas to concede that excuses could be found to cancel the Prince's engagements in Britain for the next three weeks. When Lloyd Thomas, with a face of prim misery, had left them, the Prince turned to her, and spoke with an affected casualness.

54

'There you are, Wallis, it's all fixed. I've fixed it. Genoa, Lake Como, and then . . .'

'Como will do for the moment, David.' Having until now expected to be leaving the ship here at Cannes, Wallis was dressed in a light suit.

There was a grumble of agreement from Aunt Bessie. 'I should think Como would do. No one, I notice, has consulted the wishes or convenience of' – she cleared her throat sarcastically – 'the chaperone.'

The Prince sobered at Wallis's caution. 'How wise you are.'

'From now on we must both be wise,' she told him.

'But you will come on to Como?'

'With my chaperone's agreement.'

Aunt Bessie nodded briefly.

'I couldn't be more pleased,' said Wallis.

Nor could she be, on the last morning of their holiday, breakfasting on their balcony overlooking the lake. Como would certainly do for the moment. The sunshine glinted off the water into her eyes.

She had searched for the reason why the Prince was so attracted to her, and could not find it. He liked her American directness, she knew, but beyond that? She was not a beauty, she was no longer young. In Baltimore, she would have been considered on the shelf, for good and all. And yet, here she was, sipping her breakfast coffee by a lake of legendary loveliness, with the most glamorous man in the world : a man who was not only charming, and devoted to her, but who held a golden key to a world which glittered, and excited her as nothing had ever done before, not even the fairytales of princes and princesses that her mother had read to her. For all his simplicity, his dislike of show, there was about him, even in what she called his Robinson Crusoe clothes, the aura of power. It glinted like gold. It could transmute a whim into dazzling reality, instantaneously. Resplendent hotels were glad to offer their finest suites, yachts materialized, trains and motor cars and aeroplanes waited to carry them wherever they pleased, and all

55

on the effortless turn of a head, a briefly raised finger. It was all taken to be the most perfectly natural order of things, which nothing could ever disrupt. And most incredible of all was that she, Wallis Warfield of Baltimore, had been invited into this enchanted land. She was so far from explaining it to herself that she preferred not to try, not to ask the question any more, lest she provoked the sorcerer who had conjured it up for her to grow impatient, and snap his wand.

But one question did occupy her. What happened now? She sighed, gazing over the lake. 'Home tomorrow.'

He answered as she hoped he would. 'Yes. And then what of us?'

'That is for you to say, David.'

'I don't know what to say. I don't want to promise too much, or too little.'

'Many would say that I have enough already. To be the king's favourite has always been considered an honourable position.'

'But that is exactly one of the difficulties. When I *am* king, both our positions will be quite different from what they are now.'

'You mean a prince may be pardoned for amusing himself, but a king is expected to be serious.'

'That is roughly it, yes. I am not amusing myself with you, Wallis.'

'I know that.'

'But that is how they will see it, and they will not really mind it, until I become king. Then ...' He lit a cigarette that he had been taking from his case. He breathed out a puff of smoke. Wallis waited. 'Then they will expect me to put you away, as they say.' Wallis started to say something, but he cut her off, speaking rapidly now. 'If only they would unbend. Times have changed, I understand the modern world. If only they would defy the old prejudices. If they met you they'd see your worth for themselves, see how wonderful you are.'

The Prince paused for a long time, puffing his cigarette,

before he spoke again. 'You said just now that many people would say you had enough already. Are *you* content with it?'

She did not reply, but gazed steadily across the table at his face. She was slowly turning her coffee cup to and fro in the saucer. He returned her gaze for a moment, then looked out across the lake. The sunshine glinting on the water, and on the mountain tops, was achingly beautiful.

'Could you teach yourself to be content with it?' he asked, quietly.

Still she did not answer.

Not knowing whether her silence was reflective or shocked, he asked a little more tersely, 'If this was the only way you could still have me at all, then would you be content with it?'

At last, after another pause, she spoke, in a level voice. 'Are you trying to tell me that *you* have no say in the matter? Are you trying to tell me, David, that it is this or nothing?' Was it possible, she was wondering, that the man who could summon half the world with one raised finger was not able to marry the woman to whom he was utterly devoted?

Her questions caused him to sink down a little in his chair. He leaned forward to stub out his cigarette, and said, almost mumbled, 'Custom is very strong but then again, "Nice customs courtesy to great kings".'

'What's that?' She looked up at him.

'Shakespeare. Henry the Fifth. Nice customs courtesy to great kings, Wallis.'

He sat with his hands folded in his lap, thinking. He felt an excitement start to rise in him. What was implicit in the discussion appealed to something very deep in him, deeper even than the boldness he had exhibited for nearly twenty years in defying the customs and the views of the royal household. In a very low voice, he asked himself, 'I wonder. Could I get away with it?'

'Could you what?' she asked, straining to hear him.

He went on talking to himself. 'Le Roy le veult. The

King wishes it. A new kind of royalty for a new age.'

'What are you saying, David?'

'I am saying that your wishes are not different from my wishes. And my wishes will soon be the wishes of the King of England.'

'True, my Prince.'

'Prince, yes.' He lit another cigarette. 'Not yet king.'

'So much the better. We need time, David.' She, too, was excited now, recognizing that she had prevailed over his doubts. She spoke quickly, but in a whisper, as though they were conspiring. 'You must not overdo it. Everything may be taken from us if we are too greedy too quickly, remember that. We know what we know, you and I.' She put her hand out, and rested it on his. He took her hand, and raised her to her feet, standing up with her. She was saying, 'To the rest of the world, let us be non-committal, humdrum even, for as long as may be. But when the moment comes, you will play the man.'

He put his arms around her, and spoke close to her ear. 'I will play the king.'

'And I,' she murmured, 'tell me what part I shall play, David?'

He answered by kissing her.

CHAPTER FOUR

The Prince's loneliness as a young man, and often in more recent years, had been assuaged by the one close friendship he had ever had with another man, his younger brother George, Duke of Kent. Now that too was to be taken from him, with George's marriage. As the day approached, a sadness came over him.

There was one redeeming benefit, however. At the Buckingham Palace reception before the wedding, Wallis was to be one of those presented to Their Majesties.

King George was still not well, and the draughty rooms of the Palace did not make him feel any better. The Queen had wanted him to cancel the presentation, on the grounds of his ill health. Sitting side by side with her, each on identical gilt thrones, wearing the Order of the Garter, he dismissed her anxious whispers. He had his job to do, however irksome it was. She understood.

'Mrs Ernest Simpson,' was announced. Wallis stepped up, and curtsied. As her body moved, the lights glittered brilliantly on a cluster of gems she was wearing as a brooch. The effect upon the royal pair was mesmeric. As one mind, they were asking themselves: whose money paid?

The King remembered his duty, and nodded, distantly, to the woman, receiving her at Court. Later, she was introduced to Their Majesties by the Prince. A few perfunctory words about America were exchanged, for the sake of politeness, before the King and Queen moved thankfully on to the next in the line.

The Prince wanted more for her than an official reception, much more. But it was very difficult to know exactly how to broach the subject with his parents, and exactly when, in a family that had always been atrociously unable to speak to each other about their inner feelings.

Soon, it was evident that the time was not yet. The King

was taken ill again. Recovering, he was advised that he needed a long convalescence. A suitable house had been found in the bracing air of Bognor.

'Bugger Bognor,' said the King. 'I'll do everything you tell me to, but I'll do it in London.'

The question that lay heavily on the Prince's mind was weighing on his father's also. The King would have liked to discuss Mrs Simpson with his son, but did not know how to set about it. He asked his wife, 'Has David spoken to you?'

'No.' Queen Mary knew what he meant.

'Has he perhaps asked you whether he should speak to me?'

'No.'

The King sniffed. 'He intends to speak to nobody.'

'So it seems.' The Queen, in a vaguely comforting way, started to tidy the blankets covering the convalescent bed.

The King waved her away, absent-mindedly impatient. 'For the time being, the thing can go on. He must have something like that, I suppose. But we can't allow it to stick.'

'Why not give it a few months more,' the Queen suggested, 'and then, if he has still not spoken with you, you might consult the Archbishop?' She reflected, and added, 'Or the Prime Minister?'

The King made a decision. 'I'll give him a few months more.'

Ernest Simpson was really very good about it when the Prince proposed a skiing holiday in Kitzbühl. Unfortunately, he explained, he himself was committed to spending the month of February in New York, on business, but that was no reason why Mrs Simpson should not accept the kind offer.

'Business again, Ernest?' the Prince commiserated. 'We missed you last summer.'

Ernest smiled his secret little smile. 'With respect, Sir, you'll just have to miss me again.'

'Thank you, Ernest,' the Prince said, 'you are a very generous man.' And Mrs Simpson, as she passed her husband's chair, briefly caressed his shoulder in gratitude. Simpson went to his room, and for the first time in their married life Mrs Simpson heard him slam the door behind him.

Before leaving for Austria, the Prince wanted to perform the ceremony known in his circle as 'bidding farewell to Jackson'. Jackson was the cat at the Embassy Club. On his way there, with the Simpsons, just before midnight, he bade the chauffeur stop at Lady Cunard's house, in Grosvenor Square, where a dinner party was in progress. In high spirits, the Prince swept the entire party off with him to the club.

'Just look at him,' Lady Diana Cooper remarked quietly to her husband. 'He is as charming tonight as only he can be.'

'And now is so seldom,' Duff Cooper added.

The conversation was of politics. 'The question, then,' the Prince declared after two hours of it, 'is, not who is Parliament responsible to, but who is responsible *for* Parliament?'

'You are not David, Sir, but Daniel,' Lady Cunard quipped.

'In fact, Emerald,' Duff Cooper told her eruditely, 'the idea originated with Juvenal: *Sed quis custodiet ipsos custodies?*'

'Latin!' Mrs Simpson exclaimed. 'Not my strong point.'

'Do they teach it in American girls' schools?' Duff Cooper teased her. 'Come to that, do they *have* American girls' schools?'

'*Good* girls' schools in my time,' she replied, 'were pretty much like good English ones, right down to Latin and black stockings.'

'Did you prefer the black stockings to the Latin?' Lady Cunard enquired.

'I did keep a pair by me for some years afterwards, but I must say I haven't worn them since I gave up the Can-Can.'

'That I should like to see,' the Prince grinned.

'In the bracing mountain air of Kitzbühl,' she said, 'who knows?'

As the party rose to leave the club, the Prince, with an apologetic smile, murmured in Wallis's ear, asking her to pay the bill. He never carried cash.

'I'm afraid I'll have to stop accepting your invitations out, Sir,' she laughed. 'I just can't afford it.'

'Don't forget a tip for the doorman,' he added.

Before Lady Cunard went to sleep that night, she noted in her diary, 'The little Prince talked like a prophet and drank Vichy water.'

And in her diary, Wallis wrote of 'a rising curiosity concerning me, new doors opening, interest even in my casual remarks. I am stimulated, excited, as if I were borne upon a rising wave. Now I begin to savour the true brilliance and sophistication of London life.'

The fortnight in Kitzbühl was fine, but it was not enough for the Prince. He told Hugh Lloyd Thomas to cancel other engagements. They were going on to Vienna. Yes, Vienna, 'I feel like waltzing,' and then Budapest. 'There is nothing to match the fire of the gypsy violins.'

Again, he had to wheedle, while Lloyd Thomas spoke frostily. 'Your popularity is enormous, Sir, but it does, even so, represent a limited capital. Is it wise to spend it?'

'I've fixed him,' the Prince announced to Wallis afterwards, 'but I'll have to make up for it when I get home.' He looked and sounded like a naughty boy. 'Among everything else, I must also speak to my father about you and me. I dread it, but I think I owe it to him.'

'But is he well enough?' she asked. 'He has got to get himself fit for the Silver Jubilee celebrations. I shouldn't worry him, if I were you, before you really have to.'

'But he *knows* about us, he must do, and he'll already be worrying.'

'He never worried overmuch about ... your other friendships, did he?'

'This is different. That is why I feel I owe it to him to talk to him about it.'

'I thought we agreed that we had better bide our time.'

'I'd like him to meet you, Wallis. If he met you he'd be won over.' He held her hands.

'But we have met, David. I should think very carefully before you say anything ... emphatic ... to your father.'

'But there is something to be said for coming clean. If they don't like it there's always Bertie.'

'Don't joke about it, David. You are to be King of England. None other. You.'

Time had passed, months had passed. The King knew that this friendship of his son's was different from the others, and he finally decided that he must share his anxieties with someone, in default of speaking with the Prince himself. He invited the Archbishop of Canterbury to give him advice.

The Archbishop felt obliged to start by asking, 'I suppose it is no good reminding him that this friendship puts him at risk?' He knew the answer. Since the war, young people had thought nothing of such behaviour. *Carpe diem.* It was not impossible that it might actually increase the Prince's popularity.

The King answered, 'I am less concerned with seeing my son into heaven than with seeing him on to the throne.'

The Archbishop stood at the window, his hands behind his coat-tails. He turned to face the King. 'Then we must pray only that he give her up in good time, Sir. Neither Church nor Parliament could tolerate any notion of this union becoming permanent.'

The King nodded in agreement. 'But suppose he kept her on after I am dead?'

The Archbishop abandoned any religious line of thought,

63

and gave a political answer. 'She might be acceptable ...
until he took a wife. It is, of course, out of the question
that he take her as his wife. And it would do the Crown
great damage, in almost every quarter, if he continued to
entertain her after he had married.'

'So we leave it as it is, for the time being.' The King's
conclusion was not without a trace of relief.

'We leave it, Sir. Though you will not expect me to con-
done it. As the Bard has it, "God send the Prince a better
companion." '

'God send the companion a better Prince,' the King
snorted. 'Then he would soon be rid of her.'

That wave of curiosity about her that Mrs Simpson had
noted continued to raise her up higher. Even if she could
have done anything to abate it, in line with her advice to
the Prince that they should avoid arousing drama, she did
nothing. The crest of the wave was exhilarating.

The clothes she wore were thought simple but very chic.
It was her jewellery, always growing in splendour, that was
the talk of London. Mrs Belloc Lowndes, meeting her for
the first time, afterwards declared that she found her a very
civil woman, but with one error of taste : all that dress-
maker's jewellery. At that, the ladies listening screamed
with laughter, and told Mrs Belloc Lowndes that all the
emeralds and rubies dripping from Mrs Simpson were
absolutely real. The Prince, they said, had given her fifty
thousand pounds' worth of jewels for Christmas, and sixty
thousand pounds' worth for the New Year.

When those in the Prince's charmed circle of friends
heard echoes of spiteful talk going on outside, they put it
down to pure jealousy on the part of the women he had
liked in the past, all of whom had made him, they said,
dreadfully unhappy, and none of whom had bothered even
to be faithful to him at the time. Wallis was different.

Indeed she was. At Covent Garden, in Lady Cunard's
box, she bade the Prince to hurry away at the interval,

'otherwise you'll be late joining Her Majesty at the Reception. She brushed his lapels and straightened his tie. 'There, that's better. Off you go, Sir.'

As the Prince left the box, Sybil Colefax murmured in Lady Cunard's ear, 'The Empire ought to be grateful for Mrs Simpson.'

No one in the box would have disagreed. Any outsiders who did not see that Mrs Simpson had enormously improved the Prince, who might have thought it inept to treat the heir to the throne like a schoolboy – not only were they envious of Mrs Simpson, and snobs about her being American, but above all they did not know the Prince.

That summer, there was another holiday, in Cannes, cruising to Corsica, and on, to Vienna and the fiery violins of Budapest again, and this time it was October before they returned to London. Ernest Simpson had by now been dropped, like a pilot, and was thought to have found consolation in a country cottage.

Neither Prince nor King had yet found the courage to speak to one another about it all.

'There has simply been no chance,' the Prince told Wallis. 'There was the Jubilee, George's wedding, Henry's wedding, my poor aunt's illness, the General Election, holidays . . . He has had too much else to contend with.'

'What have you in mind to tell him?'

He replied directly. 'That I have an overwhelming need of you and that I wish to bring you permanently into my life.'

She smiled, rather seriously, warmed by the sentiment, but in doubt as to the wisdom of disclosing it to the King. To help her make up her own mind, she tested his case. 'He could hardly argue with your sincerity.'

'Not on a personal level, no.'

'The King cannot overrule love.'

The Prince frowned. 'My father can overrule anything for the sake of what he sees as one's duty.'

The statement brought back to Wallis's mind the classical French tragedies that she had had to read in her last year at school. Corneille, Racine, all she could remember of them was her teacher's insistence that they proved that passionate love was the foe of duty, and to succumb to it was fatal. Out of class, the girls had discussed it among themselves, and quickly decided that they passionately disagreed. 'David,' she said, 'you say that you have an overwhelming need of me, and wish to bring me into your life permanently.'

'And I mean it. You know I mean it.'

'And you are prepared to say so to your father?'

'Yes. I rather dread the thing, but I am ready to do it. There is one comfort. My brother Bertie is much more like my father than I am, and would make a very suitable king.'

'David, you must not talk of that.' Now it was Wallis who spoke sharply. 'You must not even *think* of giving up the crown. Things may be different after your father is dead. There will be no one, then, to stand in your way.'

'Only a regiment of canting bishops and both Houses of Parliament.'

She ignored his sardonic smile. 'But you will be King.'

Now he felt the excitement that she had aroused in him at Lake Como, when she had made the same suggestion. 'And if once I were crowned . . .' he said. Could he get away with it? With Wallis beside him, those responsibilities would be easier to bear. He could almost imagine enjoying it.

She was looking hard at him. After a while, she said, 'Your father is an old man, and a sick man. Why worry him with what he will not understand?'

'If I do not speak to him, he may call on me to declare my intentions.'

'No,' Wallis said, quick and decisive. 'He will put it off for the same reason as you have. If you dread what you have to say to your father, he dreads what he has to hear from his son. If you were to decide not to go to him about it, I do not think you need fear that he will come to you.'

All her life, she had instinctively looked away from the difficult problems, hoping they would vanish of their own accord. Everyday life was thus made pleasanter, even though she had a price to pay, a recurrent ulcer, where the tensions told.

At Buckingham Palace, the King was declaring to the Prime Minister, 'After I am dead, the boy will ruin himself in twelve months. What am I to do?'

'Have you tried speaking to him, Sir?' Baldwin asked.

'So far I've followed a policy of waiting. But now that I am so unwell, I must try' – the King shook his head wearily – 'I must try to speak to him.'

'If you please, Sir. The sooner, the better, for all of us.'

'Christmas,' the King decided. 'At Christmas he will come to Sandringham.'

By Christmas, the King was haggard with illness. Spiteful tongues said that he was being hastened to his grave by the Prince's reckless behaviour: never concealing his friendship with Wallis, bedecking her with gems, and disregarding the scandal he was creating (which was fanned by those same tongues).

At Sandringham, the summons came at last. The King wished to see the Prince in his study.

'I have something to say to you,' the King said.

'Then I may have something to say to you, Father.'

The two men looked each other straight in the face. Neither spoke. The King it was who flinched, turned away. When he looked back again, he found his son's eyes had not left him. The King swallowed. 'Please,' he said, 'please be more punctual at meals. You have twice been late since you arrived here.'

'Is that all you have to say to me, Father?'

The King's voice rose in anger. 'Is it such a little thing? The clocks in this house are kept half an hour fast, by my order and my father's before me. It should be easy enough to be on time.' He stopped, and swallowed again. Gruffly, he asked, 'Did you say you might have something to say to me?'

The Prince took a breath. 'It was nothing. Just that I'd like to get in some rough shooting at Windsor after I leave here. Is that all right?'

'Of course. The ground needs shooting over. I hope that you'll continue to take an interest.'

'Thank you, Father.'

When the Prince had left, the King told his wife, 'I can't talk to him. I look into that taunting, obstinate face and I am afraid he might answer with insolence, might lightly disobey.'

'We should have found him a wife long ago,' the Queen said.

'I think not. It is better he should not marry. Neither this American woman nor any other.' His voice deepened with emphasis. 'I pray to God that he will never marry and have children, and that nothing will stand between Bertie and Lilibet and the throne.'

'Dear Lilibet,' the Queen said. 'She is not one of these modern girls, thank heavens.'

The Prince was shooting in Windsor Great Park when a letter was delivered to him. It was from his mother, asking him to return to Sandringham for the weekend. There was no immediate danger, but the doctors were uneasy about the King's condition.

By that Sunday, 19 January 1936, the Prince was motoring to London to advise Baldwin that the King's death was imminent. As the Prince left, the Prime Minister, weeping, asked him, 'Your Royal Highness, did His Majesty speak with you at Christmas, or before he began to sink? I know that he intended to.'

'Yes. He asked me to be more punctual at meals.'

Baldwin snuffled miserably.

Before he returned to Sandringham, the Prince telephoned Bryanston Court. Wallis received his news with an outwardly sympathetic calm.

On Monday evening, the bulletin on the radio announced, 'The King's life is drawing peacefully to its close.'

The Prince switched off the radio set, and returned to the King's bedroom. All the family had gathered at Sandringham, and were in the room where the King lay unconscious. The Prince's brother, Bertie, Duke of York, was upset to have missed hearing the broadcast. He had forgotten, he explained in his stammering voice, that the clocks were kept half an hour fast, and had thought he was too late.

'I'll fix those bloody clocks !' The Prince strode out of the bedroom to find Lloyd Thomas. 'Hugh !' he was shouting. In his voice there was hysteria. 'Hugh !'

'Yes, Sir?' The Assistant Private Secretary was in the study.

'Send for the clockman and have all the clocks in this place put back to the right time.'

'Now, Sir?'

The Prince screamed. '*Now!*'

Lloyd Thomas was one of the very few people who could have understood the Prince's frantic, irrational manner throughout the King's dying. It was caused not by grief, nor by remorse, nor by nervousness at his impending responsibility. It was that he had become – had allowed himself to become – a man strapped between two strong saplings tied down. And now the knot that had held them down was cut.

Lord Dawson, the royal physician, stooping by the bed, closed King George's eyes, crossed one of the hands over the other, stood back, and looked at Queen Mary.

The Queen, pale and proud, walked towards her eldest son, took his hand, bowed to kiss it, slowly straightened up, and declared, 'The King is dead, long live the King.'

In Hyde Park, the King's Troop of the Royal Horse Artillery were given the order, just after midnight. 'Fire !' The first of seventy shots of the salute boomed across London, and was answered by the Honourable Artillery Company at the Tower.

CHAPTER FIVE

More than a hundred statesmen were assembled in the Banqueting Hall of St James's for the new King's Accession Privy Council.

'When my father stood here twenty-six years ago, he declared that one of the objects of his life would be to uphold constitutional government.'

Twenty-six years ago, the old King had been 'overwhelmed' by this Accession business, on his own admission later. It was not that bad, his son found with relief. Nevertheless, the paper in his hand was trembling.

'I am determined to follow in my father's footsteps, and to work, as he did throughout his life, for the happiness and welfare of my subjects. I place my reliance upon the loyalty and affection of my peoples throughout the Empire, and upon the wisdom of their Parliaments, to support me in this heavy task, and I pray God will guide me to perform it.'

Of the affection for him, throughout the Empire, there was no doubt, as *The Times* assured him in a long leader. It welcomed 'his laughter-loving boyishness, sometimes nervous, but always self-possessed ... his tact, his kindness and sympathy, his affection for children ... his bodily activity and love of sport, his ready memory for faces, his freedom, for all his dignity, from personal or official side.' He had not spared himself, *The Times* intoned, in his indefatigable travels, his personal concern for the workers in the depressed areas he had visited. Of no king had more been expected. He would inaugurate a monarchy suited to the democratic needs of 1936, and generations after.

'All this must make no difference to us,' the King told Wallis, when they were dining together at York House in the evening of that first day.

She nodded once, carefully. It was still hard to come to terms with it all. David was King Edward VIII, and already, in the newspapers and on the radio, she sensed the intangible barriers being erected. *There's such divinity doth hedge a king.* And the man she knew was tired, agitated. She asked a simple question. 'What is to happen now?'

'For one thing,' he answered, 'we must begin to think about Ernest.'

That was not what she had meant. Ernest could wait. It was the ceremonial procedure she wished to know about.

He told her there would be proclamations in the streets. He could arrange for her to watch, from a window in St James's Palace. 'And I will join you. It will be fun, watching oneself proclaimed.' After that, there would be the royal funeral. 'We must bring my father up from Sandringham. He will lie in state. Then he will be buried.'

And then, she asked, the Coronation?

He paced the room, restless. He had heard the question, but it was vying in his mind with so many others. At length, he answered. 'There will have to be a decent interval before that is arranged. A lot of people, all over the world, must be consulted about a suitable date.'

'You will have the last word?'

'I shall be listened to.'

'You are the King.'

'Yes.'

'And Emperor.'

'Yes. Sworn, but not yet crowned and anointed.' He stopped his pacing, and looked at her. 'Wallis?'

'Yes?' She saw how vulnerable his face was.

'In all that is to come, I shall need you. Will you stand with me? And by me – will you marry me?'

After a long pause, she answered. 'There will be great difficulties for us, I think, before they will allow it.'

He took her hand in his, and gazed at it, as though reading her palm. 'Please God we may find a way through them.'

The Royal Crown was taken from its glass case in the Tower and set upon the Royal Standard that covered the

71

coffin. Behind the gun-carriage, on its procession from King's Cross to Westminster Hall, the King, in a long, heavy overcoat, plodded mournfully at the head of the small party of kinsmen and bearers. Queen Mary and her daughter, heavily veiled, followed in a carriage. The streets of London were thronged and silent. The sky was leaden.

As the procession turned into the gates of Palace Yard, a bizarre incident occurred. The Maltese cross on top of the crown, set with a huge sapphire and encrusted with diamonds, had been loosened in its mounting by the jolting of the gun-carriage : it rolled off, and fell on the road, in front of the King. 'Christ !' he exclaimed, as a company sergeant-major of the Guards flanking the coffin swiftly picked the cross up and put it in his pocket. 'What will happen next?'

'A fitting motto for the coming reign,' remarked a watching MP to his colleague beside him.

The newspapers that morning had carried a photograph of the King and Mrs Simpson together at a window, watching his proclamation.

One event in the week gave Queen Mary much pleasure. On the midnight before her husband's coffin was taken from Westminster Hall, where it had lain in state, to the burial ground at Windsor, her four sons, in full dress uniform, had descended the staircase and joined the officers already on vigil around the catafalque. For twenty minutes they stood there motionless, bowed over their swords, while the public filed past, paying their last respects. It was a gesture to captivate the popular imagination.

Some weeks later, doubts were re-entering the Queen's mind. Major Alexander Hardinge, the King's Private Secretary, a loyal and upright old soldier, complained to her that the King was neglecting his official duties, while he enjoyed himself privately at Fort Belvedere with his circle. Mrs Simpson, above all others, commanded his attention, and his choice of friends. Only the previous day, he had taken her to the races, at Plumpton of all places, while State papers were waiting for his scrutiny. When the King did finally attend to the business he could not escape, it was at times of his own choosing. His staff of appointed advisers, not to mention his domestic servants, were liable to be summoned from their beds, if it suited the King. He did not want to hear advice from any of them except when they were expressly sent for; otherwise, they were to leave him alone. It seemed that he lived in a world of his own.

There was a problem even more alarming than the King's conceit. Boxes of State papers were being left unattended at the Fort, for days, sometimes weeks, until the King could be bothered to 'grind through them', as he put it. At first he had made a great show of handling the red boxes as assiduously as he had seen his father do, but his enthusiasm had dwindled quickly. No one could be sure that the papers were secure, even that he locked them away. He would not allow any of his staff to take responsibility for their safekeeping. Who knew whether any of his friends, staying at the Fort, might not be glad of the chance to scrutinize State secrets? As Prince of Wales, the King had made no secret of his friendship with Germany, and the rise of Hitler had not stopped him making pro-German statements; when criticized, both confidentially and in public, he stuck to his opinion that he had said 'the right thing'. Furthermore, Mrs Simpson had been entertained at the German Embassy, and was thought to be on good terms with the Ambassador, Ribbentrop. What Hardinge did not tell the Queen was that, for the first time in history, the red boxes were being screened by the Foreign Office before they were sent to the King.

His attitude toward Italy was thought no sounder than his German sympathies, at the Foreign Office. Anthony Eden called on him with the information that Haile Selassie was planning to visit London, and asked if the King would receive the Emperor of Abyssinia, to signify disapproval of Italy's invasion of that country. It would, Eden said, be 'a popular gesture'.

'Popular with whom?' the King answered. 'Certainly not with the Italians.' He delivered a little lecture to Eden. The policy of trying to coerce Mussolini, which had anyway failed, was a futile one. It had only driven the Duce closer to the Führer.

'Any other policy,' Eden observed, 'would have landed us in trouble with the League of Nations.'

'It is more important to secure friends than to curry favour with a tottering League of Nations.' Eden was summarily dismissed, and the King walked back into the adjacent room, where Wallis had been waiting.

At least, Hardinge could comfort himself, the King seemed to be of a sound mind on that subject. Isolated though he was from the daily flow of informed advice and opinion that his staff would normally have offered him, he showed no signs of being misinformed about how far he could go with her. She was 'the lady of the moment'. Being American, she herself might not have understood that anything was more inconceivable; she might even have tried to use her dominant influence to persuade the King otherwise. But that was the King's problem, not anyone else's. He it was who would have to explain to her how things were done, and what things were not.

To receive his weekend guests at the Fort, the King had taken to wearing a mourning kilt. Lady Diana Cooper admired it : 'pale dove-grey with black lines, and his exquisitely fitting jacket rather Tyrolled-up in shape and improved buttons and most finely pleated Geneva bands like John Wesley. On Sunday by request he donned his wee bonnet and marched round the table, his stalwart piper behind him, playing 'Over the Sea to Skye' and also a composition of his own.' (The composition was one which his father had once heard him play; the old King had bellowed from a window, 'My advice to you is to leave this art to the Highlanders. They know what they're doing.') Wallis's taste in what she wore remained simple and chic; the jewellery with which she was adorned by the King continued to increase in breath-catching splendour, brilliant diamonds, rich rubies, emeralds glittering and winking.

74

Evenings at the Fort were passed in harmless – some said gormless – games : piling matches in turn on top of a bottle until the pile collapsed, or sitting around a raised blanket trying to blow a feather off it, all performed in dinner jackets and evening gowns. 'What would King George think of that?' the King liked to wonder, chuckling.

He was a model of hostly attentiveness to all his guests, fixing drinks, spearing olives, slicing lemons, rattling ice. To Wallis he was more than attentive. When she snagged a fingernail, he was back at her side within two minutes, panting, with two little emery-boards.

Generous to his guests, he had an extraordinary streak of meanness elsewhere. A story went around, among those who were excluded from his circle, that he had summoned his housekeeper and asked her what happened to the soap in the guest rooms after the guests had left?

'It is taken to the servants' quarters, Your Majesty, and finished up there. We all like using it up, Sir, and there's nothing else can be done with it.'

'Oh, yes there is,' the King replied. 'Soap is already provided for the servants' quarters, and charged for. From now on, the soap left by my guests will be taken to my rooms, and finished there by me. In this way, we shall not need to put out any new soap for my use.'

Such gossip seldom leaked further than those who had known the King at first hand. In the public eye, he still commanded the affection that he had brought with him to the throne. When he was in the mood, he could call upon the old energy, the royal charm, and bewitch his audience. A band of Canadian Pilgrims went home glowing with patriotism after his fraternal, old-soldier treatment of them at a memorial celebration of Vimy Ridge. His reputation for courage was confirmed when, after presenting the colours to three Guards regiments, he was riding back in procession to the Palace. In the watching crowd there was a scuffle, and a loaded revolver scuttled out and skittered under the King's horse. He rode on without flinching. Even in Glasgow, he maintained a dogged sort of charm as he performed a series of impromptu calls on private homes. 'I am your King,' he would announce at the door, but in the Gorbals' tenements he was more often taken to be the new rent-collector, and his affable smile was answered by a be-wildered distrust.

Yet, just as he was neglecting to be discreet about Wallis, so his petulance, and brittle opinions, gradually impinged upon a wider public when he was not in a mood to care. The unspeakable boredom upon his face was caught by a newspaper photographer at a presentation of débutantes: the majority of whom were not, in fact, presented, since a shower of rain had driven the King in from the Palace gar-den, and when the clouds had disappeared, so had the King. He had become adept at disappearing, once climbing out of a window at the Palace in order to escape from a tedious counsellor and rejoin Wallis. He gave offence to the congregation of Privileged Bodies – representing the Uni-versities, the City Corporation, the Bank, Canterbury, the Royal Academy, and so on – by declining to follow the old custom of receiving and addressing each deputation separ-ately.

'How many of them are there?' he demanded.

'Twenty, Sir,' Hardinge told him.

'Then the thing is the most colossal waste of time that I cannot spare.'

'These bodies are eminent, Sir.'

'So many *eminent* men?' the King asked ironically.

'Important, at the least, Sir.'

The King rejoined, 'Self-important, you mean. To save myself from death by boredom, I shall choose to receive all twenty of the Privileged Bodies together, and address one reply to the whole lot of them.'

Sooner or later, the only choice that mattered to the King had to be faced. Apart from the slowly spreading rip-ples of gossip, the King's ambiguous position with Wallis was being undermined by the collapse of the Simpsons' marriage. In the end, it was Ernest Simpson who, in his tidy and proper way, started to unravel the knot.

He called at York House. The King received him in the study, where, in plus-fours, he was practising putting, into a glass. Simpson began, 'May I be plain, Sir?'

'Truth between friends, Ernest.' The Prince's tone of flippancy was defensive, as though it were Simpson who had injured him by intruding here.

Simpson watched the ball roll across the carpet and strike the rim of the glass. 'The truth, then, is that it is time Wallis chose between us.'

'I'm sure Wallis can take care of herself.' The King retrieved the ball.

'So she has often told me. She must also choose for herself.'

The King nodded curtly, squared up to the ball, and left it short of the glass.

'I do not think, Sir,' Simpson resumed, 'that she will choose me. She is fond of me, but she is not a woman who stands by a man. If she can't have it both ways any longer, she will choose the more attractive way. Which is with you.' He spoke, as he always did, mildly but firmly.

'Aren't you being rather unfair, Ernest?'

'Truth between friends, Sir. She will choose you. What do you intend to do about it? What can you do about it, indeed?'

The King paused, in his stance, gazing at the head of the putter. 'I see what you are getting at.' He was gripping the club tightly. 'Do you really suppose, Ernest, that I would be crowned without Wallis by my side?'

Throughout the interview, neither man had looked the other in the eye, for different reasons.

Well, there it was. Now that he had said it out loud to Simpson, he had to say it again to Wallis, before it was reported to her. He told her that he had included Mr and Mrs Baldwin among the guests for a dinner party he was planning to give. 'Sooner or later, my Prime Minister must meet my future wife.' So that she should not feel obliged to comment on that immediately, he went on, 'Has Ernest spoken to you? He has spoken very plainly to me.'

'Yes, David. Ernest has spoken at last. And at length.' She clipped her speech, by way of understating the excitement inside her. 'What it comes down to is this. If I commence divorce proceedings, he will co-operate. Apart from everything else, he has found someone else.'

'Good for Ernest.'

She smiled a little ruefully. 'The someone else is an old friend of mine, Buttercup Kennedy.'

'You'll not grudge him a proper consolation? Good for Ernest, say I. And it is certainly good for us.'

CHAPTER SIX

Walter Monckton had been a friend of the King when they were at Oxford together, but now, in his Chambers, facing the King and Mrs Simpson, he seemed older than either of them, a different generation almost. As the King had explained to Wallis, behind the lowered blinds of the car taking them to the interview, Monckton was a barrister; he would advise them, and recommend a solicitor, who would in turn have to brief another barrister to speak for Wallis in the Divorce Court.

The King told Monckton the position. Mrs Simpson wanted a divorce, her husband was prepared to be helpful, but, since her name was in some quarters associated with his own, there was a risk of public comment. The King, as he explained, believed that he ought not to seek to influence Mrs Simpson in her action. Would Monckton advise her?

Monckton took it all in quietly, behind his glasses, nodding his understanding, then turned slowly to Mrs Simpson and gave her a wise, but searching, look. If, he asked her, Mr Simpson had been so helpful and considerate a husband, never obstructing her in her purposes, then why did she wish to divorce him at this particular juncture?

'I wish to be totally free of him,' she replied. 'Our marriage has gone stale, on both of us.'

Monckton considered. 'You do not need to inflict yourselves on one another. Indeed, it is clear that you do not. Why not, then, simply go your own ways, without the trouble – and possible scandal – of a divorce?'

'I may meet someone else whom I wish to marry.'

Monckton folded his hands in front of him. 'May I ask whether you have anyone particular in mind?'

Mrs Simpson did not even blink. 'I merely wish to be prepared.'

The King lit a cigarette. He was proud of Wallis's calm

answers. But when Monckton touched again, more firmly, on the possibility of a scandal, perhaps derogatory of the Crown, she turned her eyes to the King, asking for assistance.

'Mrs Simpson must consult her *own* best interests,' the King said. 'She must not allow the fact that she is my friend to dictate her course of action.' He rose, preparing to leave. Seeing Wallis rise too, he shook his head, and motioned to her to remain. 'Can I take it, Walter, that you will arrange for her to meet a reliable solicitor?'

'If you wish it, Sir.'

'Mrs Simpson wishes it, Walter. I do wish it also. Good afternoon.'

As Monckton opened the door for the King, he bowed. Then he looked sharply across at Mrs Simpson, reminding her of her manners. She rose, and performed a brief curtsey. 'Good afternoon, Sir.'

When the King had gone, Monckton remained standing. 'Mrs Simpson, before I recommend a firm of solicitors to you, there is one point on which I must be very clear. You stated that you have nobody in particular in mind as a future husband after you are divorced. You stand by that?'

'I am not getting any younger. I wish to be prepared, should the right man appear.'

'And tell me, Mrs Simpson, does the right man ever appear, in your dreams as it were, carrying a sceptre and wearing a crown?'

'It is ridiculous to imagine that I could have any idea of marrying the King.'

'Ah. Yes, ridiculous, I do agree.'

Behind his calm legal demeanour, Monckton was already deeply anxious about the outcome of the affair. He would much have preferred to have nothing to do with it – to hope it would all go away – but his obedience to the King, and his affection for his old Oxford friend, impelled him to do as his master told him, though not without expressing his doubts.

His anxiety was magnified by two meetings. At the first,

the solicitor he had engaged for Mrs Simpson told him that, after consulting his partner, he had decided that the firm would not act for her. It was too contentious.

The second meeting was with Winston Churchill, at their club. Churchill did not like Monckton's news. 'I spend my time defending the King, but if this is to happen, I shall have a very much harder task of it.' Mrs Simpson's denial that she had any intention of marrying the King was all very well, but if she was divorced the King's defenders would lose a safeguard. There would unquestionably be rumours. It was better that she stay safely married : and that the King do nothing to flaunt the friendship in the eyes of the public. 'I hear talk,' Churchill said, 'that he thinks of asking her to Balmoral this autumn.'

'He needs to have her near him,' Monckton said.

'Then let him put her with someone else nearby. Good God, Walter, kings have had close friends before without living in their pockets.'

Churchill's opinions were reported to the King by Monckton, who added that he agreed with them.

'So,' the King said, 'you would leave Mrs Simpson imprisoned in an unsatisfactory marriage simply because she is my friend?'

'I do not think she is imprisoned, Sir. What I desire is the happiest possible outcome for both of you. This may not be at all easy to achieve. It is therefore essential, when I am discussing the thing either with you or with Mrs Simpson, that we shouldn't mince matters, whatever affection I may feel personally for either of you.'

'Amen to that, Walter.'

'On we go then, Sir. How do you react to Winston's comments?'

'As for what Winston had to say about hiding my friendship – I am not ashamed of it, and I do not propose to be deceitful about it.'

'Discretion, Sir, does not amount to deceit.'

'Nor does it amount to candour.'

'Candour does not insist that private relationships be made public property.'

When Monckton did manage to find a solicitor, Theodore Goddard, who was willing to take on the business, Mrs Simpson did not congratulate him. 'It was hardly a labour of Hercules, surely?' she asked.

'It has not been easy, Mrs Simpson.'

'You are trying to tell me that I am untouchable by the legal profession?'

'No, but very, very hot to touch.' In any case, Monckton added, the London divorce courts were booked up for some time ahead. She should consult Goddard when the holiday season was over.

'But that is weeks away,' she said. 'If money can do anything to hasten...'

'Divorce is a cumbrous matter in this country, Mrs Simpson. Very silly and oldfashioned of us ... is it not?'

As it happened, the law's delays were no inconvenience to Mrs Simpson. She would be away on a summer cruise with the King.

No word of the divorce had yet reached the King's staff. But word of the holiday did, and sent Major Hardinge hurrying round to Buckingham Palace, where the Queen was still living. 'He is very restless, Ma'am, unusually so.' Hardinge waited to see if the Queen had any theory about that, but she merely shrugged, so he continued. 'He wanted to go to the South of France for a holiday, but the Ambassador in Paris objected : with the strikes there, and the Red Flag being flown, so we hear, and the civil war in Spain, it would be unwise for the King to stay in France. So now His Majesty has hired a yacht of Lady Yule's, the *Nahlin,* for a Mediterranean cruise.'

'And *she* goes too?' the Queen asked resignedly.

'Mrs Simpson goes too, Ma'am.'

'If he were true to himself, if only he were, he could perform his task so well.'

'There is something new going on, Ma'am. I am not yet sure what it is, but there is a new element in the affair. This restlessness of His Majesty's, it seems different from his normal state.'

'It's not boredom, by any happy chance?'

'No, Ma'am. On the contrary. He seems excited, but I do not know the cause of it.'

Anthony Eden called at York House to discuss the itinerary of the King's cruise with him. He said he was grateful that the King had accepted the Paris Ambassador's advice. 'As you know, Sir, our constitutional custom does rather discourage the monarch from airing his sentiments on politics.'

'Have I been airing my sentiments, Mr Eden?'

Eden hesitated. 'You have made some of your sympathies very plain, Sir. For example, your leaning towards Mussolini's Italy.'

'I just want him to be given a fair chance, to see how he gets on.'

'To many people, Sir, it is already plain that he has a somewhat brusque mode of getting on. Too brusque for democratic comfort. And this brings me to a request for which I must entreat your earnest consideration.'

'Well?'

'I'm informed that Your Majesty will be sailing down the Dalmatian coast.'

'With your permission, Mr Eden.' The King smiled thinly. He outlined his political route: calls on General Metaxas in Athens, and Kemal Ataturk in Istanbul.

'But you plan, I believe, Sir, to board the yacht which you have chartered at Venice?'

The King nodded, and restlessly tapped a paper-knife on his desk top.

'Which,' Eden said, 'would mean travelling through Italy.'

'Ah.' The King understood. 'Mussolini's Italy.'

'Quite so. Please think better of it, Sir. You will offend a lot of people if you go there.'

'Will I?' said the King challengingly.

At that, Eden sat up straight, and looked hard at the King. 'Your loyal subjects, Sir, are proud of you.'

The King met Eden's reproachful eyes. The two men studied each other. It was the King who flinched. Quietly, he asked, 'Where should I join the yacht, then?'

The answer was, to travel in a private carriage on the Orient Express through Switzerland and Austria to Jugoslavia, where the *Nahlin* waited for them at Sibenik. Also waiting for them were enormous crowds of the people of Dalmatia, and a gang of American newspapermen. Twenty thousand people, dressed in their native costumes, saw them off from Sibenik, and the cruise down the coast became a triumphal progress at every port. The King and Mrs Simpson were delighted by the welcome that the simple, spontaneous crowds gave them. They might, on reflection, have taken alarm. For what the crowds were triumphantly shouting was not only 'Long live the King!' but also 'Long live love!' – *Zivila Ljubav!* Their simple hearts, briefed by the American newsmen, were going out as much to Mrs Simpson as to the King. The feelings that the couple shared between them were becoming public property even in a kingdom remote from England.

The King could see quite clearly that the people's eyes were not focussed on him alone. 'I suppose,' he teased Wallis, 'you think this is for me?'

'Of course. Who else?'

'You're wrong,' he told her, smiling. 'It's all for you – because these people believe a king is in love with you.'

'David, this is madness. If you're not more discreet, you'll have everybody else knowing that.'

'Discretion is a quality which, though useful, I have never particularly admired.'

Not unaware of the shutters clicking wherever they went, whether alone in a small boat or on the bridge of the yacht passing through the narrow Corinth Canal, the King stripped to the waist in the hot sunshine every day. He was in a high, holiday mood, swimming, picnicking, driving golf balls into the sea from the deck of the *Nahlin* : until one incident changed it, one tactless remark from Godfrey Thomas, in attendance as Assistant Private Secretary.

After dinner on the boat one evening, when the servants had been dismissed and the party was relaxing over coffee and liqueurs, Duff Cooper asked the King how he had found General Metaxas.

'Friendly,' the King replied. 'And inquisitive about all the things which my Foreign Secretary tells me I should not discuss with strange men. Or even with my own friends.'

Diana Cooper asked, 'Was he offering any information about Greece?'

'No.' The King smiled impishly. 'There was one topic I tested him on, but he kept mum. I asked him about King George of the Hellenes and a certain friend of his. A married friend. A lady.'

Only good manners covered up the awkwardness that the King had stirred around the table. Perhaps he was unaware of it; or perhaps he was so infatuated that he did not care. He went on smiling while the company discussed the absence of any speculation in the Greek newspapers about the affairs. Then Mrs Simpson asked the direct, American question. 'Is he in love with the lady?'

'So they say, Wallis,' the King told her.

'Then why doesn't he marry her?'

The awkwardness was now palpable, but it might still have been smoothed away by a display of British social team-work. It was Godfrey Thomas who decided to make a matter-of-fact reply. 'Because the King of the Hellenes may not marry a woman who is a commoner and married to another man.'

The King's smile had congealed on his face. It was a mask of displeasure.

He did not speak for several minutes. His tactful friends eagerly steered the conversation on to the sights they might see the next day. What were the plans for the day? They looked to the King. His mask had not melted.

'Sir,' Thomas asked again, 'what *are* the plans for tomorrow?'

The King leaned toward Mrs Simpson. 'Wallis, what are the plans for tomorrow?'

No one enjoyed the rest of the cruise. No one was allowed to enjoy it. The King did not wish it. He sulked relentlessly.

As the *Nahlin* approached Istanbul, Duff Cooper was glad the trip was over. 'Until Thomas made that remark,' he said to his wife, leaning beside him on the rail, 'it was Prince Charming with his Cinderella, playing to the plaudits of a peasant chorus. But then it was brought home to him that he is not in a pantomime. There is no fairy godmother to gloss over the social disparities, and he must be steered, not by a Dandini in tights, but by Mr Baldwin in his baggy tweed trousers.'

'You don't think,' Lady Diana asked, 'that he might still be listening to Dandini? Planning a marriage of romance?'

Duff Cooper shook his head. 'Unless infatuation has quite robbed him of his wits, he must know that he cannot have it both ways. He must relinquish the woman, or the throne.'

Back in London in early September, the King's first duty was to call on his mother, at Buckingham Palace. After describing the diplomatic episodes of his holiday, he bade her goodnight with the news that he intended to spend the last two weeks of the month at Balmoral. In return, she kissed him on the forehead, fondly. That the monarch should spend that fortnight at Balmoral, attended by senior members of the Cabinet, the Church, the Services, and the House of Lords, was a century-old tradition. She was comforted to see him honouring the old ways, and went to bed with a more hopeful heart.

A few minutes later, Mrs Simpson took a telephone call in Paris, where she was spending some days on her way back from the holiday. It was the King, asking if her cold was better. No, she told him, but she had more serious matters to worry her. She had caught up with her accumulated mail, and it was full of clippings, sent by friends in America, from the papers and magazines over there. The United States, it seemed, was seething with speculation about Wallis Simpson of Baltimore, and her friendship with King Edward of England. There were photographs of their summer together that would fill an album. That the speculation was wild and inaccurate did nothing to allay her anxiety.

He soothed her. 'I've been through all this before. It's just American newspaper gossip. It doesn't mean a thing.' There was nothing at all about it in the English press, he said. It would all die down in a week. Meanwhile, she was to get rid of that cold. It would not do to arrive at Balmoral with a sneeze.

'You'll ring again?' she asked.

'Tomorrow. Without fail.'

The next morning, there was a tedious business to get through, meeting Hardinge and Thomas to plan the King's diary for the following weeks.

'So,' Hardinge said, 'that is settled, then, Sir. When you return from Balmoral, it will be to take up residence in the King's Chambers in Buckingham Palace.' He ticked off the item on his agenda. Her Majesty would be pleased to have that arranged, he thought to himself, even though it meant that she would have to move out of the Palace and into Marlborough House.

The King lacked enthusiasm. 'I suppose I must move in there, sooner or later.'

Hardinge nodded efficiently. 'When you return from Scotland. Now, the guest list for Balmoral, Sir.' He took a paper from the sheaf he held, and handed it to the King, who had chosen an armchair rather than to sit at his desk.

The King looked down the list, then took out a propelling pencil and began to write in some more names. 'We'll add Mr and Mrs Herman Rogers,' he said, naming some

87

old American friends of Mrs Simpson's. 'And Mr Esmond Harmsworth. And' – he looked up at Hardinge, with a frown of enquiry – 'I don't see Mrs Simpson's name here.'

Hardinge looked above the King's head. 'I understood, Sir, that for Balmoral' – the stress on *moral* might have been thought a pun from anyone but Hardinge – 'you would be retaining your father's guest list.'

'So I shall, Major Hardinge, so I shall. But with some leavening of the exalted dough.' He added the name of Mrs Ernest Simpson, and handed the list back to Hardinge. 'By the way, please would you make sure that the full list of my guests at Balmoral is published in the Court Circular. Thank you.'

Hardinge went straight to tell the Queen, his mouth still tight with outrage. 'I only hope, Ma'am, that the American papers won't make too much of it.'

The Queen's voice, when she answered, was low, and hard. 'They've made hay with what they've already got.'

Hardinge sought to console her. 'Very few of those papers can have found their way to England so far. But more will do so, I fear, if it goes on. And this . . .' His outrage reasserted itself. 'Fort Belvedere is one thing, Ma'am. Balmoral is another.'

'What about the English newspapers?' the Queen asked.

'They are being exceedingly discreet, Ma'am.'

'So far.' The Queen was staring down at the floor, slowly shaking her head. Suddenly, reaching a decision, she fumbled in her reticule and withdrew a copy of the *New York Woman* which she thrust at Hardinge. 'Page fifty-three,' she muttered. While he thumbed through it, she was saying, 'Just above an advertisement for women's hose.'

Hardinge was reading the item. *As an interesting instance of Royal privilege, be it noted that if Ernest Simpson should wish to divorce his wife, the King cannot be sued for adultery in England.* When Hardinge looked up again, a tear was running down each of Queen Mary's cheeks.

* * *

In the great granite pile of Balmoral, the daily routine had not altered since Victoria's time – breakfast from the sideboard, deer-stalking at ten until dusk, dinner rounded off by five pipers marching round the table. Afterwards, there were games of cards, or – a concession to the twentieth century – a makeshift cinema in the ballroom.

Mrs Simpson was due to arrive a week after the King had been installed there. He announced that he was going to meet her himself, at Ballater station.

Thomas, however, was there to remind him that 'Your Majesty will be opening the new hospital buildings in Aberdeen at the time Mrs Simpson reaches Ballater.'

'Aberdeen?' the King asked, in a raised, petulant voice. 'That engagement was never finally agreed. I said, when they asked, that I might still be in mourning.'

'But, Sir,' Hardinge joined in, 'they know very well that you are not still in mourning. Your recent holiday had no air at all of mourning about it.'

The King's face was creased up with impatience. 'My brother, the Duke of York, will go in my place.'

'With respect, Sir,' Thomas said, 'the Duke of York is not the King. It is the King they will be waiting for in Aberdeen.'

'I tell you,' the King shouted, 'the King is still in mourning for his father!'

Hardinge's answer came swiftly and crushingly. 'Then so is his brother the Duke of York.'

'I had my way.' There was a trace of pride in the King's voice as he told Wallis the story, motoring in the royal car back from Ballater. 'Bertie will be coming in later to tell us how he got on at Aberdeen. I think that he, and others, are starting to receive the signals I'm putting out. That if they are for me, then they must also be for you.'

The ambiguity in those signals was brought home to them that same evening. As the King stood in the hall at Balmoral, receiving his guests, Mrs Simpson was standing with him, only just perceptibly to the rear.

The Duchess of York made a slight curtsey to the King.

He leaned forward, to greet her with a kiss on the cheek. 'Wallis Simpson of course you know,' he said. Mrs Simpson bobbed a little curtsey to the Duchess, who ignored her. The King's face, as he watched his sister-in-law walking away, was a mask of frustration.

'Shush,' Wallis whispered to him, and shook her head slightly, indicating that he should take the offence calmly. Then she bobbed again, to the Duke of York, and smiled discreetly. 'Good evening, Your Royal Highness.' She turned, and slowly, with dignity, followed the Duchess.

As the Duke shook hands with his brother, he told him, in his stammering voice, that he had been seen meeting Mrs Simpson at Ballater.

'A man must have his private life,' the King replied.

'A private life, I suppose, is very much the privilege of a p-private man.'

By 1 October, the King was back in London. He called at Monckton's Chambers, to enquire about the progress of the divorce suit.

Goddard had all the papers prepared for Mrs Simpson, Monckton told him. 'He hopes to keep it all as far as possible out of the public eye. But it is inevitable that there will be talk of . . .'

'Of my friendship for Wallis,' the King said brusquely. 'Well, they must take me as I am, Walter. A man different from my father, and determined – *determined* to be myself.' Monckton started to shake his doubtful head, but the King insisted. 'Of course I shall be available for public business when I am wanted. But my private life must continue to be my own.'

'In your case, Sir, private and public cannot help but overlap.'

'I can and shall lead my private life as I did when I was Prince of Wales. Unobserved, at the Fort. In peace. I need to rest.'

'And,' Monckton enquired dubiously, 'when you come up to the Palace?'

'The Palace.' The King sighed. 'It smells, did you know that, Walter? Musty. Dank.' He stood up, and looked out of the window, his hands in his pockets. 'I hate the Palace.'

CHAPTER SEVEN

Stanley Baldwin had also been on holiday that summer. He had badly needed the rest from the responsibilities he had to bear in 1936 : the civil war in Spain reverberating on British relations with Germany, Italy, Russia, America; Hitler's occupation of the Rhineland, and the Franco-British attempts at appeasement; the Italian capture of Addis Ababa, to which the League of Nations had resigned itself. At home, the spectre of unemployment could not be exorcized : the slump had put two-and-a-half million out of work, and the queues for the dole-counter and the soup-kitchen seemed to stretch intractably into the future. The only political beneficiaries were Oswald Mosley's Black-shirts.

And now, waiting for him on his desk when he returned from his holiday, Baldwin found two huge trays overflowing with a problem from which his staff had thought it better to shield him until he had rested. One tray was full of cuttings from the American press : colourful, fulsome accounts of the uncrowned King's friendship with Mrs Simpson, and hundreds of photographs of the pair of them together on the beach, in a boat, walking, motoring, among crowds of onlookers. The other tray was crammed with letters from British and Commonwealth citizens living in foreign parts, who, unlike their cousins at home, had seen all the publicity, and disliked it so much that they felt obliged to write, polite or scandalized, to Downing Street, Canterbury, the Palace. Baldwin sat down, and read the stuff for most of the morning. When he had finished, he pushed the trays away, and sat with his head in his hands. Then he asked his secretary to call the Archbishop of Canterbury.

Surely, the Archbishop asked when he arrived, the Prime Minister had some inkling about it all earlier?

Baldwin admitted that Major Hardinge had tried often enough to alert him, but he had always assumed that it would prove to be another of the King's passing infatuations. 'And I had this consolation : as long as Mrs Simpson remained married to Mr Simpson, no *constitutional* issue could arise. A scandal we might doubtless weather. That is what I felt when the old King mentioned the affair to me just before he died. But if any public notion were to gain ground that the King might wish to *marry* a previously married woman ...'

'You still have that consolation,' the Archbishop told him.

'Well, we are more or less safe for the present. But the King's appetite for her company becomes more flaunted every day.' Baldwin gestured at the overflowing trays. 'It grows by what it feeds on. Unless it be contained, it must burst into scandal.'

Not far from Downing Street, at Theodore Goddard's offices, Mrs Simpson was listening to her solicitor's account of the progress of her divorce suit. Evidence of Simpson's adultery with Buttercup Kennedy had been obtained by a private detective peering into an hotel bedroom at a moment when the couple were lying side by side in bed. But, Goddard explained, there was a difficulty : the adultery had been witnessed in a room of the Hotel de Paris at Bray, and the most convenient court for the case, since the detective and hotel staff lived nearby, would have been Reading —

'London,' Mrs Simpson interjected, 'would be more convenient to me.'

— but Goddard continued, Reading Assizes were not taking divorce cases, the London courts were booked up for more than a year, and thus, if his client wished to expedite the case —

'I do.'

— it would have to be put down for hearing at Ipswich, 'which,' Goddard concluded, 'is convenient to no one.'

Mrs Simpson sighed. She was just in the process of moving house in London. A furnished, four-storeyed house by Regent's Park was being prepared for her, and meanwhile she was staying at Claridge's. Now, this meant another domestic set-up. 'I shall have to take a house in the area of Ipswich to comply with the residential qualification.'

'I congratulate you,' Goddard said, 'on your knowledge of the law.'

'My knowledge of divorce, Mr Goddard. What I really don't like is this. Ipswich will make it all look hole-and-corner. I do not seek publicity, but I don't want to seem to be evading it, and Ipswich will give that impression.'

'Dear lady,' Goddard reassured her, 'by engaging a barrister as distinguished as Mr Norman Birkett κc, we automatically refute any charge of trying to do things on the sly.' Or, he thought to himself, on the cheap.

At Downing Street, after the Archbishop had left, Baldwin's attention was called to foreign affairs by the arrival of Eden. The Foreign Secretary had taken the initiative in applying an embargo on the supply of arms and aircraft from Britain to either side in the Spanish war. To sell to one side and not to the other would, Eden argued, expose Britain to reprisals, and to sell to both sides would provoke the accusation of cynically exploiting the civil war. The problem arose, he went on, taking another sheaf of notes from his parliamentary secretary, of how to enforce the embargo on firms who were keen to sell their arms. To solve that problem, it was necessary to examine the commercial mechanisms. The transactions were normally arranged covertly in neutral territory. It was, therefore, often difficult for British agents to detect just . . . Eden became aware that Baldwin had been standing at the window, with his back turned, for some minutes. 'Prime Minister,' he asked, 'forgive me, am I boring you?'

'Tiring me.' Baldwin thumped his hands down on the window-sill. 'Tiring me.'

Eden rose, and nodded to his secretary that it was time for them to leave. As they reached the door, Baldwin turned. 'Anthony.' Eden gently pushed the secretary on toward the door, but himself stayed behind. When the secretary had left them, Eden saw that the Prime Minister's usually cheerful face was drawn, almost haggard. 'Tell me,' Baldwin asked, 'have you received any correspondence about *the King*?'

Eden nodded, reluctantly. 'Yes, I have, a great deal. But in view of what is going on in Europe, I have tried to believe that the matter is not worth my attention.'

Baldwin answered in a querulous voice. 'It won't just go away, you know.' He rested, his hands on the back of a chair, then continued more soberly. 'We may have difficulties there.' He gave Eden a self-pitying smile. 'I hope that you will try not to trouble me too much with foreign affairs just now.'

Eden was astounded, and much put out. The international situation had come to such a pass that the Home Office had started to issue instructions about the use of gas-masks, and to put them on display so that the populace would be familiarized with them. And here was the Prime Minister asking his Foreign Secretary not to bother him with foreign affairs, because of a tawdry affair of the King's. He looked carefully at Baldwin, to convince himself that the man was in a fit condition to continue this conversation, let alone the government of the country. 'What,' he asked eventually, 'do you propose to do about the King? Teach him his duty?'

Baldwin shook his head with vehemence. 'He shouldn't need teaching, not with the upbringing he's had.'

'But clearly,' Eden said, 'you believe he does need it.'

'And if he won't listen?' Baldwin's knuckles were white where his hands gripped the chair.

'Have you spoken to him?'

'I think of doing so, all the time. And I dread it.'

Eden reflected. 'You once told me that he had invited you to remember always that you could speak to him about anything.'

'That's right.' Baldwin seized gratefully on the memory.

'On a train, when he came back from Africa in a hurry because his dad was ill.'

Eden nodded encouragingly, as though to say, that solves it, then. But he saw that the gleam of hope in Baldwin's eyes had been transitory. The Prime Minister was shaking his head again, despondently. He did not look like the very tough politician he was reputed to be. Was this third term of office going to prove too much for him?

Taking his leave, Eden saw a way of bringing together their separate concerns. 'If foreign affairs follow their present trend, we shall need a sound man sitting on the throne.'

Baldwin was back at the window. 'I only pray that we may have one,' he said.

The ripples were spreading outwards. They did not have far to spread. Within a mile radius of the window where Baldwin stood, in the heart of London, were a handful of rooms in which one man could take a decision that might affect the whole of Britain, and the opinions of the British people. Among these estates of power were numbered the newspaper offices. One was *The Times*, whose opinions commanded attention because the Editor, Geoffrey Dawson, was known to be on terms of confidentiality with the government. Another was the *Daily Express*. Although it was the most popular newspaper of the day, its opinions, like those of its sister paper the *Evening Standard*, were regarded as the idiosyncratic obsessions of the proprietor, Lord Beaverbrook. Nevertheless, it had a greater power than that of mere opinion, namely disclosure. Hence it was that a telephone call, in which Beaverbrook told Goddard that he knew about Mrs Simpson's divorce action and proposed to publish a statement, brought Goddard, accompanied by Monckton, hurrying to the office in Fleet Street.

Monckton went on to the attack at once. 'Very well, the King's friend is getting a divorce from her faithless husband. Leave aside her right to privacy, which I don't for one moment expect you to recognize ...'

In the eyes of Beaverbrook, as he lit a large cigar, was a cold gleam of dislike for Monckton. It alarmed Goddard. Anxious to avoid antagonizing the press baron, he interrupted. 'Leave aside all that,' he said reasonably, 'and instead consider this : granted the King's friend is getting a divorce, this would be news only if she were doing so in order to become yet friendlier with the King.'

'And what,' Beaverbrook asked behind a cloud of blue smoke, 'makes you think she isn't?'

'I have her personal assurance,' Monckton said emphatically, 'that she has absolutely no intention – she has no *conception* of marrying the King.'

'That will not stop people from imagining she has,' Beaverbrook answered.

'Is what people imagine news?' Goddard asked.

'What the King's friend imagines is.' Beaverbrook shrugged sceptically. 'Perhaps she is telling the truth.'

'Do a favour to an old friend, Max,' Goddard said, 'sleep on it.'

Beaverbrook puffed at his cigar, grinning.

There was nothing in the *Express* the next morning, Goddard saw with relief. At least the Beaver had slept on it for one night. But it was imperative to warn the King. He went to Buckingham Palace, again with Monckton.

The King had been feeling sanguine about the divorce since speaking to Birkett, the barrister. The unpleasantness through which Mrs Simpson would have to sit in the court had preyed on his mind, and Birkett, he hoped, might be persuaded to mitigate it as much as possible. The barrister, touched by the King's obvious devotion to Mrs Simpson, assured him that it would be a very straightforward case. When the King worried about 'collusion' – the possibility that someone might show that Simpson and Buttercup Kennedy had deliberately been witnessed together at Bray, and that the case might thereby be nullified – Birkett calmed him again. The judge, he said, would almost certainly award a decree *nisi*, meaning that a period, probably of six months, would be allowed for objections : but who would object, since it was a known fact that Simpson intended to marry Buttercup Kennedy? She was not just a woman hired for the legal occasion.

The news that Goddard and Monckton brought did not apparently upset the King. Monckton advised, 'Send for Lord Beaverbrook, Sir, and make it clear that, while you have no desire to stop him reporting the proceedings in court, you would deprecate any sensational attempt to whip up attention in advance.'

'Send for His Lordship, did you say?' the King smiled. 'Rather, let's say a friendly telephone call and an invitation to a quiet drink. After all, the press barons are a formidable crew. I don't want another Runnymede on my hands.'

Beaverbrook professed himself charmed by the King's invitation, but begged to be excused for two days because he was 'heavily engaged with my dentist'. Hanging up, Beaverbrook wrote the appointment in his diary for Friday, 16 October, just below another appointment he had, to meet Mr Ernest Simpson.

Stanley Baldwin was at Buckingham Palace, waiting to speak to the King. The matter to be discussed was His Majesty's review of the Fleet, at Southampton in November. It was a routine matter : but any matter concerning the King, especially one over which they had to meet each other, now filled Baldwin with dread. If only the King himself would raise the matter which chiefly preoccupied both of them, if only the King would break the ice, then Baldwin could have taken the plunge. But ... How easy, in retrospect, it had been to serve George v. One always knew exactly where one was. Baldwin felt sorry for himself : that he should happen to be Prime Minister at the moment when this unprecedentedly embarrassing king had to be dealt with. Where was he, anyway? Hardinge had made some excuse about a telephone call that the King had had to take. Baldwin looked at his watch.

Hardinge, waiting by the door, decided to make use of this opportunity. Since the King would not confide in him directly, it was his duty to press others to bring the King to his senses. He had hoped that Her Majesty would win the day, but it seemed that she had less influence upon her eldest son than he had expected. Baldwin, then, was the best hope. Hardinge cleared his throat. 'Sir, I am afraid I must so far presume as to ask you to raise another subject with the King, after you have discussed the review of the Fleet. I think you know what I refer to?' He waited for a reply, and saw that he would not get one. Baldwin was staring at a Canaletto over the mantelpiece as though it had transfixed him. 'Prime Minister,' Hardinge resumed, 'the day will come very soon when you will be forced to intervene in the matter. I must beg you to address yourself to it now, before you are compelled to.'

Baldwin spoke at last, apparently addressing Canaletto. 'As long as Mrs Simpson remains married, we have a formal safeguard.'

Hardinge answered in stern monosyllables. 'We do not know how long that may be.'

Now Baldwin's face registered his feelings : lame, wretched. 'For some time now I have been thinking almost continuously of this predicament, Major Hardinge.'

'With respect, Prime Minister, it is time to compose one's thoughts, and to act upon them.'

Baldwin stroked his forehead. 'I had hoped that the problem might be staved off, until after the Coronation.'

Hardinge would not relent. 'That is more than seven months away. And' – his voice had begun to inflect rhetorically – 'even if the King were duly crowned, how could that help us, if he still preserved his inclination for Mrs Simpson?'

'What exactly *is* his inclination there?'

'I believe it is increasingly obsessive, Sir. If' – Hardinge broke off, hearing the brisk steps of the King in the corridor. He gave Baldwin an urgent look. 'You *will* speak to him?' he asked in a low voice.

As Baldwin bowed to the King, and received a gesture to seat himself again, he would have realized, had he not been fighting down fear, that there was something strained in the manner of the King, too : someting too exaggeratedly casual. 'Shall you be long, Mr Baldwin? I've just received a message and find I must go to Sandringham.'

Hardinge read the signs, and, unseen by the King, was staring at him with barely disguised hostility.

'I shan't be long, Sir,' Baldwin said; and, snatching for any kind of support, added, 'It might be convenient were Major Hardinge to remain with us, to help us spot any snags in the arrangements.'

'No,' the King said. 'I would like you, please, Alex, to arrange for a car to run me down to Suffolk.'

'Norfolk, Sir. Sandringham, you said,' Hardinge answered, with some relish in the correction.

'What's the odds? East Anglia.'

'Shall you be out of London for long, Sir?' Baldwin asked.

'Only till tomorrow afternoon.' The King fidgeted. 'Alex, please would you see about that car at once.'

Hardinge bowed, and withdrew. With him went any intention on Baldwin's part to broach the matter of Mrs Simpson today.

When he had finished with Baldwin, the King told his chauffeur to drive him to Felixstowe.

Walking hand in hand with Wallis along the desolate beach, he commiserated with her having to spend weeks here, in a tiny house, on her own, except for the cook, and the maid. But, until the business at Ipswich was done, it was better that she should not visit London often, where she would be recognized, and fan public curiosity.

'You will come and see me often?' she asked.

'They are watching me, Wallis. Waiting for me to put myself finally in the wrong. I think they would like to be rid of me.'

'You are imagining things, David. They can't get rid of you, with your popularity in the country. Your being here can do no harm.'

'I have to go back tomorrow.' He explained his appointment with Beaverbrook.

'But why . . .' she started.

'*Please*, Wallis.' What she could not understand, she really would have to take on trust, from him.

He left her with a promise to return on Monday.

The King stated his case to Beaverbrook cogently but calmly. All his concern was for Mrs Simpson. The thought that notoriety could surround her divorce was distressing her to the point of illness. Notoriety attached to her only because of her association with himself, through the publicity accorded to her being a guest on the *Nahlin*, and at Balmoral. (Publicity, Beaverbrook thought to himself, that the King had, to put it charitably, done nothing to deter.) 'I thus have a duty to protect her,' the King argued. 'Will you assist me?'

'In what way, Sir?'

'In the way of reticence.' And the King went on to ask not only that comment be suppressed in advance of the divorce hearing but also that, after it had been reported, there should be no undue speculation.

'There is bound to be public interest, Sir, in the future of the lady.'

'But less if you use your influence to discourage it.'

'That must depend, Sir, on there being nothing spectacular in store for her after her divorce.'

Wearily, but with relief at having brought Beaverbrook round, the King reiterated, 'Nothing spectacular is in store for her after her divorce.'

Beaverbrook, who had been a threat, was now an ally. His influence was brought to bear on the other newspaper bosses, who consented readily enough to respect the King's wishes. Esmond Harmsworth was pleased to do so, having been a member of the King's circle at Balmoral and elsewhere. Only Lord Kemsley was a bit sticky, voicing his suspicion that the King might, after all, be intending to marry Mrs Simpson. When told that the King knew he could not do that, Kemsley grumbled, 'Does he? He seems pretty fond of his own way to me.' However, in the end Kemsley felt unable to stand apart from the rest of the press, at the risk of attracting the despisal of the nation. 'I suppose,' he allowed, 'one has to believe the word of one's own King.'

Kemsley's doubts had been sown on the same day that Beaverbrook interviewed the King. He had joined a weekend house-party at Lord Fitzalan's house in Windsor Park, where his fellow guests were the Duke of Norfolk, Lord Salisbury, and Stanley Baldwin. The conversation inevitably turned around the matter that haunted Baldwin's mind and was concentrated by the arrival of Major Hardinge, wanting to speak with the Prime Minister. They withdrew into the study.

Hardinge had now heard about the divorce suit, and knew the date of the hearing. 'October the twenty-seventh, of this year. That is, ten days from now.'

Baldwin stared at him. A decree *nisi* for six months would become absolute at the end of April, leaving the King time to marry Mrs Simpson before his Coronation, in May. 'Surely,' Baldwin said, 'he can't even dream of it. It would destroy him. He could not be crowned.'

'What if, in spite of everything, the country still wanted him?' Hardinge asked.

'The Archbishop would not crown him.' Baldwin ran a finger around his wing-collar.

'With respect, Sir,' Hardinge said, 'the position can be contained if you will insist to the King, first, that the divorce suit be dropped immediately, and second, that he cease to be so indiscreet in his friendship with her.' Baldwin had slumped down in a chair. Hardinge's voice ground pitilessly on. 'The King will be at Fort Belvedere until tomorrow at noon. You could telephone him there to arrange an appointment.' Baldwin's mouth was moving, but no words came out. 'Prime Minister,' the loyal major told him, 'if these divorce proceedings are not halted, the danger to His Majesty, to the Crown itself, will grow more terrible with every day that is allowed to pass.'

Baldwin peered up at the ring of noble portraits staring at him from the walls of the study. 'Very well, Alex. I will telephone His Majesty tomorrow morning.'

It was not so easy. When Baldwin telephoned the Fort, he was told the King had gone to Sandringham. At Sandringham, they told him that His Majesty had not arrived yet. Baldwin, not ungrateful for one day's remission, thereupon called Hardinge and asked him to take over the pursuit, and arrange an audience for the following morning, Tuesday.

Hardinge kept telephoning to Sandringham, and discovered that the King had sent word that he would be arriving very late that night. Where, then, was he now? No one said, and everyone knew. Hardinge asked that the King be informed that his Private Secretary and his Prime Minister had both been trying all day to reach him on urgent business, and would telephone again in the morning.

It was four o'clock the next morning when the King finally arrived at Sandringham, but by nine o'clock he was telephoning Hardinge, to ask what the urgent business was. As he listened to the answer, his face tightened, and his breathing grew more rapid. 'No. Mrs Simpson's divorce is Mrs Simpson's business,' he said tersely. 'It is not a matter in which the Prime Minister may intervene.'

'But *you* may do, Sir,' Hardinge answered. It was not difficult for him to picture the expression he had provoked on the King's face.

'Let me repeat,' the King said in a cold rage, 'Mrs Simpson's divorce is Mrs Simpson's business.'

'But, Sir, the Prime Minister ought at least to have the benefit of hearing you discuss the situation. He had hoped to see you urgently yesterday. With great respect, Sir, you must receive the Prime Minister today. He will come to

Sandringham, if you wish. But he does want to keep the appointment entirely private.'

'Very well.' The King's voice had risen a little with desperation, under Hardinge's relentless artillery. 'I would sooner see him on my own ground. Tell him I will receive him tomorrow morning – yes, tomorrow, at ten o'clock at the Fort.'

The King replaced the receiver, and sat staring at it. His fists were clenching and unclenching. His mind was travelling beyond tomorrow's interview with Baldwin, into the future : or, rather, the several possible futures.

CHAPTER EIGHT

The Wednesday morning was misty. When Baldwin arrived at the Fort, he was told that the King was in the gardens, and invited Mr Baldwin to join him there. A footman led him out, through the gardens, calling 'Your Majesty!' Baldwin followed on, noting the beauty of the grounds. He could start by complimenting the King on his gardening.

The King was smiling a greeting when they found him. Baldwin praised the arrangement of the grounds, and the King began to talk enthusiastically of all that he had done to the place since he had found it. They paced slowly along together, examining rhododendrons, roses, hydrangeas, azaleas, until Baldwin shivered. 'It's chilly out here, Sir. I beg your pardon, but could we go inside and have a drink?'

In the study, the King gestured toward a tray of drinks. 'Please help yourself, Mr Baldwin.'

Baldwin picked up a glass and a decanter of whisky. 'You first, Sir. Say when.'

'Thank you, Mr Baldwin, but I never take a drink before seven o'clock in the evening.'

'Oh,' was all Baldwin could find to say in reply. He poured himself a stiff whisky, and sat in the chair to which he was motioned. The King hesitated, then sat down too.

Baldwin took a sip, and started. 'Do you remember, Sir, how we once had dinner on a train together – you were returning from Africa – and you said then that I could always speak frankly to you about anything?'

'When I was still Prince of Wales.'

'And now you are King, Sir. And now' – Baldwin spoke as tranquilly as he could – 'there is a lady in the case. Does what you said on that train still hold good?'

The King's face was blank. 'It must do, since I said it. Well, Prime Minister?'

Baldwin opened his mouth, but decided to take a gulp of

whisky before he went on. There was still a long way to go. 'The country is in transition, Sir,' he resumed, 'between the old age and a new.'

'The country is always in transition between one age and another,' the King answered unhelpfully.

'Quite, Sir. You are the sovereign we need to see us through *this* transition.'

The King replied with a patient politeness. 'It is very civil of you to say so, Mr Baldwin.'

Baldwin took another mouthful from his glass. 'You have all the advantages a man can have. You are still young. You have had the fine example of your father.'

Over the King's bleak expression a slight wince flickered.

'You are fond of your house, and your splendid garden. You are known to be fond of children. Everything about you inclines your people to love and to trust you, as indeed they have done since you were only a boy. But the years do go on, Sir, and now you have one disadvantage. You are not married, and you ought to be. And because you are not married, there is rumour.'

'What rumour?' the King asked. 'Where?'

'Everywhere.' Did he really not know? 'Not in this country so much, or not yet, but in America, Europe, the Dominions : rumour that you are seriously bound to – a certain lady.'

'It is true I have a friend.'

'Rumour makes more of it, Sir. Rumour is dangerous. It can be lethal.' Baldwin paused. He had made a start. After a sip of whisky, he continued. 'May I remind you, Sir, of what I have said to you and to your brother in the past. The British monarchy is a unique institution. Today, it stands for far more than it has ever done in all its history. It is the last link of Empire. It is, in this country, the guarantee against many evils that have afflicted other countries. In the last three generations, enormous respect has grown up for its integrity. But, if this kind of rumour is allowed to do its work, that respect could dwindle, and vanish, Sir, in a tiny fraction of the time that was needed to establish it. It could vanish in a matter of months, or even weeks, Sir. And once it was gone, I doubt if anything could restore it.'

The King's eyes were wry. Quietly, he asked, 'All this because the King has a friend?'

'You may think me Victorian, Sir. You may think my views out of date. But I believe I know the mind of the British people, and I say this: although standards are lower since the war, *because* of that, people expect a higher standard from their King.'

Baldwin drank down what was left of his whisky. He looked at the tray of drinks, but decided against it. Instead, he put his glass down, and reached into his pocket. First he brought out his pipe, which he laid on the arm of his chair. Then he reached into his wallet-pocket, and produced a large envelope. He took out a sheaf of letters and press-cuttings, and handed them, without speaking, to the King.

The King's expression, as he glanced through them, was first rueful, then impatient, and finally disgusted. It was true he had known there was newspaper gossip abroad – Wallis had mentioned cuttings that Aunt Bessie had sent her – but he had had no idea how far the muck had spread.

'And now,' Baldwin was saying, 'the American papers are full of stuff like this.' He passed over another sheet: the word DIVORCE was prominent in the headlines. While the King gazed at it, Baldwin added, 'Even the Chinese vernacular papers too, Sir.'

The Chinese vernacular papers were the last straw. The King angrily crumpled the pile together into a ball, strode across to the fireplace, and hurled it onto the flames. 'We need some fresh air,' he announced. 'The sun has broken through now.' He walked quickly out to the gardens again.

Baldwin picked up his unlit pipe, and trotted after him. He had to push the point home at once. 'You can burn those, Sir, but all the time there's more of it pouring off the presses, sapping the position of your throne. I do not believe, Sir, that you can get away with it.' He was proud to have prepared that phrase, knowing how often it was on the King's own lips.

It stopped the King in his tracks. 'Get away with what? What do you mean, Prime Minister?'

'I think you know our people, Sir.' Baldwin stepped carefully along the path between two flowerbeds. 'They'll tolerate a lot in private life, but they will not stand for this kind of thing in the life of a public personage.'

'What kind of thing?'

'Well, for example, when they read in the Court Circular of Mrs Simpson's visit to Balmoral, they resented it.'

'The lady is my friend. I do not wish to let her in by the back door, but quite openly.'

Baldwin put his empty pipe into his mouth, and sucked it. Now, it was his turn to be silent, while the King made some explanations.

'That is a private decision for me, Mr Baldwin. As to my public duties, I hope you will agree that I have carried them out with dignity.'

'I do agree, Sir.' Baldwin felt unable to deny the King the softening stroke he was asking for. 'And all the more so as I know that the duties of royalty are not much to your liking.'

'I know there is nothing kingly about me' – the King waited, but Baldwin would not oblige him again so soon – 'but I have tried to mix with the people and make them think I was one of them.' Baldwin was still sucking his pipe. The King concluded, lamely, 'Very well, then, Mr Baldwin, what more can be said?' He turned to face the Prime Minister, who gazed past him at the view of Virginia Water.

'This much more can be said, Sir.' Baldwin nerved himself. 'Must be said. This coming divorce is what rumour feeds upon. Sir, cannot you have the case put off?'

'Mr Baldwin, the case is the lady's private business.' The King was on familiar ground, and his voice grew prouder in consequence. Baldwin's heart began to sink again, as the King repeated the formula, with all its awful implications of a tragic crisis to come. 'I have no right to interfere with the affairs of an individual. It would be wrong were I to attempt to influence Mrs Simpson just because she happens to be a friend of the King.' He turned, and walked back into the house with an air of having said the last word. Baldwin stood still for a moment, clutching his pipe, a portly, wretched figure again. Then he followed.

'Say when, Mr Baldwin.' The King was pouring his visitor a second whisky. As he handed it to him, he was solicitious. 'You look tired, Mr Baldwin. Shall I send for your car?'

Baldwin held up his hand to stay the King. 'There is yet more to be said, Sir.'

'Oh yes?' The King stood waiting, reluctant to resume a conversation he had thought finished, or to invite Baldwin to sit down again.

Wearily, with deliberation, Baldwin started once more. 'If you will not halt this divorce case . . .'

'I have told you, I have no right to.'

'. . . then there will be, almost certainly, a decree *nisi*, and six months of – six months of suspense, Sir, the very thing which feeds rumour fattest. The press cannot be expected to keep silence on the matter indefinitely and once they begin to repeat the rumours a most difficult situation will arise. There might be sides taken, and factions grow up in this country, in a matter where no factions ought to exist. The rumours might be quelled, Sir, if Mrs Simpson left the country. Should a decree *nisi* be awarded to her, cannot you ask her to go abroad for six months?'

The King faltered. 'For Mrs Simpson, England *is* abroad.' Then he smiled, with a spreading gesture of his hands, suggesting something that could not be helped. 'She is our guest, Prime Minister. She is *my* guest.' He hesitated again, then decided he wanted Baldwin to know the explanation of everything. His smile became radiant. 'Wallis is the only woman in the world for me, and I cannot live without her.'

The tender exaltation in the King's voice depressed

Baldwin. There was nothing to say in the face of such emotion. But hold on, he thought: what exactly was the King telling him? *I cannot live without her.* He could not say that unless it was his intention to marry the woman. In that case ...

To the King, Baldwin's frown of curiosity, as those thoughts were passing through his mind, had the appearance only of a vulgar scepticism in response to his declaration for Wallis. He was offended, and impatient to get rid of this bore. 'I will send for your car,' he said abruptly, and pulled the bell-rope by his desk.

The ordeal had drained Baldwin, but he found the energy to pursue this most vital point of all. 'Sir,' he began, 'I –.' But he was cut off by a footman opening the door. The King asked for the Prime Minister's car to be brought round at once. Well, Baldwin thought, he had made a start, at least. There would be another day to make a finish of it.

The King had taken him by the elbow, as though Baldwin were a very elder statesman, and was steering him toward the door. 'I fear you are tired, Mr Baldwin. So, for now, let us just agree on this: that you and I must settle the matter together. I will not have anyone else interfering.'

All the old charm was back, and Baldwin nodded in appreciation. To have got even so far filled him with such relief that he could happily have gone to sleep for a week.

Unfortunately for Baldwin, he was allowed scarcely a catnap after lunch before Major Hardinge insisted on seeing him, with the Archbishop, to hear what the King had said. Baldwin's account left them thoughtful, but dissatisfied. They were particularly intrigued by the King's moment of exaltation. Hardinge repeated it aloud, as though it were a crossword clue. 'Mrs Simpson is the only woman in the world for me, and I cannot live without her.'

' "Wallis",' Baldwin corrected him. 'In his emotion he called her "Wallis".'

Hardinge shrugged impatiently. 'But what did he mean?'

While Baldwin readdressed himself to the questions of the morning, the Archbishop pressed him. 'Did you not ask him?'

'Not in so many words,' Baldwin said. 'I tried to lead him into elucidating, but he was evasive. He was tired, as I was. So I left. I had, after all, achieved what I went for. I had warned him about the rumours, and I had broken the ice.'

'But,' Hardinge persisted, spelling out the measure of Baldwin's failure, 'you had not asked him whether he had any notion of marrying her.'

Baldwin massaged his temples. 'From his earlier answers, I doubted that he had any such notion.'

'Everywhere there are *doubts*, Prime Minister,' Hardinge said.

'I could try to resolve them,' the Archbishop offered, 'if he would see me.'

Baldwin was glad to let someone else have a go. Hardinge approved, too: 'The sooner Your Grace warns him *firmly* of the dangers in entertaining the faintest idea of marriage, the better for all of us.'

Nettled by Hardinge's remark, Baldwin felt it was time to score a point. 'Should not someone warn *her*, also?'

After a pause for reflection, that idea won approval, too. Theodore Goddard would be asked to make sure his client fully realized that for her to marry the King was utterly inconceivable.

The first stratagem misfired. The King refused to see the Archbishop. 'We agreed, Mr Baldwin, that you and I would settle this by ourselves.' He did not tell Baldwin that he had disliked the Archbishop intensely since the day after George v's funeral, when the Primate had clumsily tried to curry favour with the new King by assuring him that he had often defended his behaviour against the old King's hostility.

As for Mrs Simpson, she received Goddard's mission derisively. 'Very well, Mr Goddard, if you insist I will say it once more. The very idea of my marrying with your King is in every way ridiculous. Now, will *that* stop these rumours?'

'No, but it will reassure His Majesty's friends.'

By the time His Majesty's friends had received that reassurance, they were faced with the *New York Journal*:

KING WILL WED WALLY

While the Archbishop sat staring glassily at the paper's headline, Hardinge filled in for him what the text said. 'It goes further than any of those rags has done before now. It states unequivocally that the King will marry Mrs Simpson, that after the Coronation she will become his consort.'

'At least,' the Archbishop remarked, 'they seem to be letting us off having her as Queen.'

'I wouldn't be altogether sure of that,' Hardinge said. He leaned over the Archbishop's shoulder, and jabbed a finger at a passage. The Archbishop read it out aloud. '*King Edward believes that the most important thing for the peace and welfare of the world is an intimate understanding and relationship between England and America* . . . What deplorable prose,' the Archbishop commented.

'And what a deplorable prospect.' Hardinge's moustache twitched ironically.

The Archbishop read on. '. . . *and that his marriage with this very gifted lady may help to bring about that beneficial co-operation between English-speaking nations.*'

'But gentlemen,' Goddard intervened, 'Mrs Simpson told me again only yesterday, with her own lips, that any idea of her marrying the King was ridiculous – her word, and by no means the first time she has used it on the subject.'

Hardinge rapped the *Journal*. 'This kind of sludge, leaking into the country and contaminating opinion, can still do untold harm. Furthermore, it must gall the British papers, who have promised to keep quiet.' He looked to Goddard. 'They will stick to that?'

Goddard gave his opinion in the tone of a lawyer's argument. 'They made that agreement in good faith, on the strength of information supplied in good faith, that there was no possibility of a marriage. But, if they should ever have reason to suppose that the information was misleading, then clearly they could claim that they were released from their treaty.'

Monckton was sent to see Beaverbrook and Harmsworth again. They repeated their acceptance of the King's word that he did not intend to marry Mrs Simpson, promised quiescence in their own papers, and their continued influence on the rest of the press. There was one risk, that a paper wishing to spring ahead of its rivals might jump the gun without warning; but the penalties, after the sensation had died down, could be dire – the scorn of readers, the disapproval of advertisers, and the peril of putting just one foot the wrong side of the libel laws. If that risk could be discounted, there remained one emigna : *The Times*. Neither Beaverbrook nor anyone else outside government was in a position to give undertakings about what attitude Geoffrey Dawson, the Editor of *The Times*, would adopt. All Beaverbrook could say was that he knew for a fact that Dawson was eager to make a statement on the matter.

Dawson confirmed that, when Monckton took him to lunch at their club. '*The Times* should make its position clear,' Dawson asserted. 'It should sum the known facts, make calculations as to the possible outcome ...'

Monckton interrupted. 'They would be speculations, Dawson.'

'... calculations, Monckton, calculations. And *The Times* should then provide serious comment from both the moral standpoint and the constitutional one.' He patted his mouth with his napkin. 'The trouble is, that we of *The Times* are ashamed.'

'Ashamed to raise the matter?'

'Ashamed of the matter which we should be raising. Look at this, Monckton.' He brought out a bulky envelope, and handed it across the table. 'Here is a letter which I have this morning received from a British resident in the United States. It is very far from being unique, except perhaps in its prolixity.'

Monckton, having looked through the letter, asked if he might take it to show Baldwin. Dawson agreed, but said that he would go with him to Downing Street.

The letter Baldwin read, while the other two watched him and waited, referred to 'the poisonous publicity attending the King's friendship with Mrs Simpson' which 'gravely lowers British prestige in American eyes'. The writer had deeply admired the King when he was Prince of Wales, and had 'looked forward to the day when he would bring a new vision and a new inspiration to the task of kingship. In common, I fear, with a great many others, I have been bitterly disappointed. The doings of the King, as reported in the American press, have in the course of a few months transformed Great Britain, as envisaged by the average American, from a sober and dignified realm into a dizzy Balkan musical comedy attuned to the rhythm of Jazz.' In contrast to George v, the monarchy was now 'filled by an individual who has made himself the subject of cheap and sensational gossip ... unsavoury gobbets of news ... a perfect avalanche of muck and slime ... The prevailing American opinion is that the foundations of the British throne are undermined, its moral authority, its honour, and its dignity cast into the dustbin.' After many more pages, the writer concluded, 'nothing would please me more than to hear that Edward viii had abdicated his rights in favour of the Heir Presumptive, who I am confident would be prepared to carry on in the sterling tradition established by his father.'

When Baldwin at last looked up from the letter, Dawson asked, 'Can you wonder that we of *The Times*, reading such things every day, are ashamed?'

'What shall you do?' Baldwin asked. 'The other papers will take their lead from you.'

'I shall do whatever you wish me to do, Prime Minister.'

Baldwin answered very quietly. 'I wish you to do nothing.'

*   *   *

The following day, at Ispwich, Mrs Simpson gave evidence that her husband's manner to her had been indifferent for two years, that he had been going away for weekends alone in spite of her complaints, and that she had finally discovered that his absences were spent not on business matters but with a lady. She was awarded a decree *nisi*, to become absolute in six months. Costs were against Simpson.

She had not been able to sleep the previous night. Now it was over, she stood in the corridor of the court, while Birkett and Goddard offered their congratulations.

Monckton came rushing up, to warn them that a vast crowd including many newspapermen, was outside. He had directed Ladbroke, the King's chauffeur, to wait with the royal car at the rear entrance. Hurrying back along the corridor, Birkett murmured to Goddard, 'The dogs have found. The vixen breaks from cover.'

And the scent of the royal car was rich. The hunt was in full cry around it by the time Mrs Simpson and her party got there. A police cordon held back the crowd. At the appearance of Mrs Simpson, news-cameras flashed. Two of them were at once seized by the police and broken underfoot. As the car drove away, the police forcibly held back the reporters who tried to pursue it.

That night, the King and Mrs Simpson had dinner together to celebrate. He told her about his meeting with Baldwin, but, 'Don't be alarmed,' he said. 'I'm sure I can fix things.'

Baldwin and Hardinge studied the newspapers together the next morning, and found that the editors had all kept their word. The court proceedings at Ipswich were formally reported, and nothing more. Baldwin was particularly relieved, having heard about the eager mob outside the court.

'Well,' Hardinge commented, 'the King did send his own car for her. If he goes on behaving like that . . .' He remembered the letter that Dawson had brought to Downing

Street, which had been forwarded to the King. Surely that would have served to remind him that his time was running out. He could not expect the press to keep silence for ever. He had to make his intentions plain, to the whole kingdom.

Baldwin shook his head. 'There will be more and more reporters, and sooner or later there will be something like this.' He handed across a cable from the Washington Embassy, which reported a selection of the headlines in the American press.

Hardinge looked through it with distaste, and read aloud: KING'S MOLL RENO'D IN WOLSEY'S HOME TOWN. He had to smile. In any tragedy there was always a vein of the comic. 'I never knew Wolsey came from Ipswich,' he remarked.

'Quite a coincidence,' Baldwin agreed. 'Wolsey had to deal with a lot of royal intrigue of this nature. Things were easier for him, of course, than they are for us. He could shut awkward people up in the Tower. That's where I'd like to put her.'

'And where,' Hardinge enquired, 'would you put *him*, Prime Minister?'

CHAPTER NINE

The skies turned against the King. What was known as
'Queen's weather' – fine days for State occasions, enjoyed
by the monarch since Victoria's time – betrayed Edward VIII
on 3 November, when he opened Parliament. Nevertheless,
there were many who stood in the pouring rain for a
glimpse of their popular King, as he rode in the gilt coach,
drawn by eight greys. They were disappointed. The King
decided that pageantry in the rain was implausible, and he
rode to Westminster in a closed Daimler. He could not
wear a crown yet, before his Coronation, and so he had an
admiral's cocked hat on his head as, in the House of Lords,
he swore to maintain the Protestant faith – a vow required
by the Constitution, but made with distaste.

What struck those watching the ceremony was the boyishness of the King's appearance. He looked, one said,
'exactly as he did in 1911 at the investiture at Caernarvon.
Not a day older, a young, happy Prince Charming.'

Mrs Simpson was not enchanted by the description. 'A
pretty little prince?' she drawled. 'If he did still look like
that, he'd be a monster of retarded development.'

'Chips' Channon rebuked her. 'You don't have to take it
so literally, Wallis.'

'Ah,' she sighed, 'I'm taking everyone literally these days.
It comes of spending so much time with lawyers, you
know.'

'Never mind,' Channon consoled her. 'That's all over
now.'

So it was, she agreed. And yet, she said, she could truthfully wish that it had never started. After all, she told Channon, it was all Ernest's fault, really. But for his insistence,
she would never have divorced him.

The remark surprised Channon no less than it did those to whom, like the assiduous gossip he was, he repeated it.

When Walter Monckton was summoned by the King to call on him at Windsor Castle, he imagined it would be for another consultation on how to handle the press barons. Given another dozen guesses, he might not have made the right one.

'It is time I made myself quite plain to you, Walter,' the King began. 'You have been our closest advisor for months.' He was restless in his chair, and now rose, and stood by the window, looking over the park. Monckton watched him, puzzled. Then the King turned to face him. 'I mean to marry Wallis.'

Monckton dissembled the shock of surprise, merely nodding slowly, twice. 'That,' he said, 'is not quite what she gave me to understand, Sir.' He thought of his exchanges with Mrs Simpson and of the many times he had, in good faith, reassured the press barons that this was not her intention : he felt himself cheated by what the King had said.

'Whatever may have been said in the past, I mean to marry her.'

Monckton nodded again, as though quite understanding. He was a man who would have nodded understandingly at a firing-squad. One thing he did need to understand immediately. 'Does she mean to marry you, Sir?'

From anyone else, the implication would have thrown the King into his most petulant display. For Monckton, a proven friend, he controlled himself. 'I *shall* marry her.'

'Not for six months, at any rate, Sir.' There was some comfort in that, he thought.

He was wrong. 'But much sooner than that, I must make it clear to everyone that, once the decree is absolute, the marriage will take place.'

'Would it not be wiser to say nothing yet, Sir? There is no need to commit yourself before April.'

'But I am already committed in my heart, Walter.' The King shook his head solemnly. 'Honour requires that I say so aloud. I cannot go forward toward my Coronation knowing that I intend this marriage, and not letting it be known to the Government and people of my country.'

You will not get away with it, Monckton wanted to warn him. You have, just this week, sworn once again to uphold the Protestant faith, of a Church that will anoint you King, but does not, will not, recognize divorce. How can you even hope to square that circle? It is not merely a religious question : the people of this country, whether or not they are churchgoers, will not be on your side. They could not idealize you, after hearing that. But no, now was not the tactful time to say such things, Monckton decided. He would, rather, continue to counsel a waiting game. If everyone, and especially the King, could only learn a little patience, there might be time for a miracle to hatch. Carefully, he asked, 'Then when *will* you let it be known?'

'It is very difficult, Walter. There is so much at stake.'

'The simple question,' Stanley Baldwin said, 'is this : what does His Majesty intend?'

Neither of the two men discussing the matter with him at Downing Street could tell him.

'There is no simple answer,' Hardinge replied.

Clement Attlee, leader of the Labour Party, asked, 'Major Hardinge, you don't think that the King will be content merely to carry on with this woman as his friend?'

Hardinge shrugged. 'I just don't know, Major Attlee.'

'Because in that case,' Attlee thought, 'if he is discreet and the press forbearing, the thing might be contained for a time.'

Hardinge told him that not everyone took that view. On their own initiative, certain highly placed civil servants had prepared a draft statement for Baldwin to submit to the King. Neville Chamberlain had re-drafted a version which, though less peremptory, still asked the King to terminate his association with Mrs Simpson 'forthwith', on pain of the National Government's resignation.

'That is too drastic,' Baldwin remarked, tamping tobacco into his pipe.

'It also suggests,' Hardinge added, 'that "this distasteful matter" – Chamberlain's phrase for it – could easily be settled if Mrs Simpson were to leave the country.'

'He won't have that,' Baldwin observed, behind a cloud of smoke. 'He made that quite clear to me the other day.'

Hardinge sniffed at the smoke, in disapproval of the complaisance behind it.

Attlee asked if he might see the draft, and a copy was passed across to him. He read it through, and, in his brisk manner, commented at once. 'I agree. This talk of resignation is too drastic as yet.'

'As yet?' Hardinge asked. 'How long do we give him, then? Till Christmas? Till the Coronation? How long, Major Attlee? Mr Baldwin?'

'He must be warned, not bludgeoned,' Attlee said. 'Urgently warned that, unless he puts a stop to it, he will bring a crisis on himself and all of us.'

Baldwin saw Attlee and Hardinge to the front door of No. 10 himself. He did not want them to enter into conversation with his next caller, Dawson of *The Times*. He knew that Dawson had come about the same matter. It might be unwise to let the leader of the Opposition realize that, in spite of the war in Spain and the deteriorating situation in Germany and the slump at home, the Prime Minister's time was now devoured by His Majesty's love affair.

Dawson was calling as spokesman for several newspaper editors. In return for remaining silent about the King, they wanted Baldwin's assurance that the Government had the matter firmly in hand.

'You have my assurance,' Baldwin told him.

It was not enough. 'You know,' Dawson asked, 'that two affidavits have been filed requiring the King's Proctor to intervene in the Simpson divorce?'

'Yes,' Baldwin said, 'I know. On grounds of alleged collusion.' It was, he told Dawson, not an unwelcome development. If there were an intervention and the decree *nisi* were not made absolute, Mrs Simpson would still be married to Mr Simpson, which would stop the gossip about her marrying the King. The matter would revert to what it had been, a romance, and 'romances,' Baldwin stated, 'are more perishable than marriages.'

'So we may hope,' conceded Dawson, 'but meanwhile the press are bound to comment soon.'

Baldwin sighed. 'The Cabinet, Mr Dawson, is watching all aspects of the situation very carefully. We have the matter in hand.'

'*Firmly* in hand, Prime Minister?'

Baldwin put his pipe in his mouth and nodded. Dawson was still looking at him. Baldwin rose to conclude the interview.

While the King was at Southampton, reviewing the Fleet, Major Hardinge sat at Buckingham Palace, drafting a letter to His Majesty. Several discarded drafts were already ashes on the fire. It was not easy to write all that he had to say while trying to discipline all that he felt. But, as the King's Private Secretary, he saw it as his paramount duty now to warn the King more severely than Baldwin had managed to do.

The pressures were not tolerable any more. There were the opinions on the King's behaviour that Baldwin had been taking. Attlee had confirmed that the Labour Party would not stand for it – not just the Parliamentary Party, but the broad spirit of nonconformist opinion throughout the land. Citrine of the TUC had confirmed that, with an acerbity sharpened by what he had read, and heard, on his recent trip to the USA. Sinclair, the Liberal leader, was no more complacent. There was the statement drafted by the civil servants and Chamberlain, which was now to be considered at an emergency meeting of the inner Cabinet. The

King's Proctor was being invoked. Most serious of all, in Hardinge's loyal eyes, were the intimations he had received of opinion in the Dominions. Lord Tweedsmuir, the Governor-General of Canada, had written confidentially to Hardinge about the dismay that people there, especially young people, would feel if their 'idol' were besmirched : particularly when the smirching had in it an American element. The monarchy set the standards of conduct in Canada; it was 'the one stable centre' in a godless world, and Canadian families were 'in dread of anything which might weaken that stability.' There was in Canada, furthermore, a truly 'personal affection' for the King : any offence to their loyal devotion would be received as a grievous personal loss. And Tweedsmuir had more right than most to intuitions of that sort, Hardinge reflected as he looked at the letter again : as a younger man, John Buchan, he had hymned the virility of a younger Empire. Australian opinion was congruent with the rest. Stanley Bruce, the High Commissioner, had told Hardinge over lunch that day : 'if there is any question of marriage with Mrs Simpson the King would have to go, as far as Australia was concerned'. Hardinge had urged Bruce to go and tell Baldwin that, which he did, forcefully; the 'madness' should be stemmed at once, by telling the King that to contemplate the marriage could lead only to his being forced to abdicate, by popular demonstrations against him. If the King took no notice of that warning, Baldwin and the Government would have no choice but to resign.

Hardinge was still considering his letter to the King when Dawson called to see him. Dawson had also been drafting a statement on the matter, for a leading article in *The Times*. He did not, he told Hardinge, intend to publish it straight away; but the press could not hold back much longer, and when the dam broke it must be *The Times* which spoke first. Dawson showed Hardinge what he had written. In return, Hardinge, desperate for a second opinion on his letter, showed it to Dawson, who gave it his entire approval.

Whereupon Hardinge put the letter in an envelope, and addressed it to His Majesty at Fort Belevedere.

All the way back from Southampton, the King was looking forward to having a bath. He had never deserved one more. His visit to the Fleet had been attended by incessant rain. The long lines of men drawn up for inspection had been soaked through before he had set foot on deck. Waterproofs had been produced for the inspecting party. While Hoare, the First Lord of the Admiralty, got into his, the King declined to wear one. Soon, he was as drenched as the men. It endeared him to them, as he knew it would. They smiled, pleased, loyal. He had not lost his touch. Nor his memory – every officer and every rating in the Fleet he seemed to know by name. He enjoyed himself as much as the men did. Away from politicians, stuffy staff, gossips, he could be the cynosure of a crowd who respected him and liked him : above all, a crowd with whom he had a feeling of fraternity, because of his naval education. It was a rare and warmly grasped opportunity for him to share the exaltation of spirit that, for months, had brought him no reward but guilt. These faces were smiling for him and Wallis.

He excelled himself at a smoking concert in the aircraft carrier *Courageous*. Only a handful of officers were allowed to join him and thousands of ordinary seamen. He dominated. He played his charm like a stringed instrument. Moving freely through the crowd, he broke up any lingering formality by starting a community sing-song to the accompaniment of a seaman's mouth-organ, conducting the massed chorus himself :

> *A Yankee ship sailed down the river,*
> *Blow, boys, blow.*
> *A Yankee ship sailed down the river,*
> *Blow, my billy boys, blow.*

The response was hearty and enthusiastic. Jumping back onto the platform, he made a brief speech that brought the house down, and won him three cheers that might have been heard in Buckingham Palace.

And so, as he descended from the Daimler and walked into the Fort, he was anticipating his bath with the glow of a tired man who knows he has earned a comfort. Afterwards, Wallis would be waiting for him in the drawing room, with Aunt Bessie, who was over on a visit to see her niece through the divorce business. As the butler helped him take his coat off, the King told him, 'I'm going straight up for a bath, Osborn. Tell the ladies I'll join them when I'm more presentable.'

'Yes, Your Majesty. Ah, Major Hardinge asked me to tell Your Majesty that there is a letter for you in the study which he is most anxious you should read without delay.'

'A letter from Major Hardinge himself?'

'So I understand, Your Majesty.'

The King glanced to right and left – bathroom or study, comfort or duty? – and resigned himself to reading Hardinge's letter first. 'Damn,' he was muttering, 'oh, damn. Osborn, please tell someone to draw my bath, and let me know as soon as it's ready.'

'Very good, Your Majesty.'

The envelope on top of the red boxes was marked *Urgent and Confidential.* The King tore it open.

Buckingham Palace,
13th November, 1936

Sir,

With my humble duty.

As Your Majesty's Private Secretary, I feel it my duty to bring to your notice the following facts which have come to my knowledge, and which I *know* to be accurate :

(1) The silence of the British Press on the subject of Your Majesty's friendship with Mrs Simpson is *not* going to be maintained. It is probably only a matter of days before the outburst begins. Judging by the letters from British subjects living in foreign countries where the

Press has been outspoken, the effect will be calamitous.

(2) The Prime Minister and senior members of the Government are meeting today to discuss what action should be taken to deal with the serious situation which is developing. As Your Majesty no doubt knows, the resignation of the Government – an eventuality which can by no means be excluded – would result in Your Majesty having to find someone else capable of forming a government which would receive the support of the present House of Commons. I have reason to know that, in view of the feeling prevalent among members of the House of Commons of all parties, this is hardly within the bounds of possibility. The only alternative remaining is a dissolution and a General Election, in which Your Majesty's personal affairs would be the chief issue – and I cannot help feeling that even those who would sympathize with Your Majesty as an individual would deeply resent the damage which would inevitably be done to the Crown, the cornerstone on which the whole Empire rests.

If Your Majesty will permit me to say so, there is only one step which holds out any prospect of avoiding this dangerous situation, and that is for Mrs Simpson to go abroad *without further delay*, and I would *beg* Your Majesty to give this proposal your earnest consideration before the position has become irretrievable. Owing to the changing attitude of the Press, the matter has become one of great urgency.

I have the honour, etc., etc.,

ALEXANDER HARDINGE

P.S. I am by way of going after dinner tonight to High Wycombe to shoot there tomorrow, but the Post Office will have my telephone number, and I am of course entirely at Your Majesty's disposal if there is anything at all you want.

As the King read through the letter, a pulse in his temple had begun to throb. His mouth and cheeks had drawn tight in fury, and desperation. He sat gazing at the sheet of paper, shocked by its sudden storm, and enraged to be advised to banish from his own realm the woman he intended to marry. It was so cold, so cold. How could any man in love be addressed like this? How could Hardinge, even Hardinge, be so crassly unfeeling? *Was* it Hardinge? Or was it not perhaps someone putting Hardinge up to it? Who, then? Who but Baldwin? And those nebulous, sinister figures who circled behind the Prime Minister? Why were they doing this to him? Why did they so hate him, and Wallis? Why?

'Sir ... Sir ...'

Through the red mist, the King became aware that his butler had been calling him. His bath was ready.

That evening, he said nothing to Wallis about the letter. He wanted advice on it first. And besides, she had enough to put up with. The Fort had become a kind of weekend sanctuary to her, where she was protected from the spiteful gossip and malicious eyes of their enemies, and their friends.

He telephoned Monckton, who agreed to meet him at Windsor Castle on Sunday afternoon. The unusual appointment he vaguely explained to Wallis as urgent business, but he could not hide his trepidation.

'You need a rest,' she said. 'Tell them you're ill, that you've taken cold in all that rain.'

Aunt Bessie chided her. 'To plead false sickness, Wallis, is to tempt Providence.'

'Quite right, Mrs Merryman,' the King agreed. 'But tell me, how does one placate Providence?'

'By telling the truth, I guess.'

'Let us hope it is really so simple,' said the King.

On Sunday, when Monckton had read the letter, the King asked him whether all this talk about the Government resigning could be true?

'It could be true, Sir. But not quite yet, I think.'

'So Hardinge is trying to force the issue?'

'It would be more accurate, Sir, to say that he is trying to force you to face the issue.'

'To force me to send away the woman I love. They misjudge me, Walter. They are striking at the very roots of my pride. It is a challenge, that letter. Very well, I am not such a faint-heart that I shall not meet it.'

'Hardinge's letter is too blunt, Sir.' How else could it be, Monckton thought to himself, between two men so different, and two men, moreover, who have had so little to do with each other outside the formal business appointments laid down by the King for their meetings?

'You think he is *wrong*?' the King asked.

'I think,' Monckton temporized, 'he is lacking in sympathy.'

'So do I. I cannot trust such a man. I will not put my confidence in someone who bullies me in this insolent manner. Walter, will you be my advisor from now on?'

'I already am, Sir.'

'I meant, take Hardinge's place.'

Monckton, a political animal, at once saw the error. 'You must not dismiss Hardinge, Sir. If you do, it will become known that you have had a breach over Mrs Simpson. You must retain him and be patient, Sir. However, if you wish, what I can do is go between you and the Government from now on.'

'I do wish. Thank you, Walter. I know whose side you are on. Now then. Hardinge says I should send Wallis away. We agree he is too blunt. But could he be right?'

Monckton sat back, and took it carefully. 'It would put an end to crisis, if not entirely to scandal. Some would say it is your duty.'

The King's head jerked. 'Do you say that?'

Monckton temporized again. He reminded the King that, in this very room, and only a few days before he had declared that he meant to marry Mrs Simpson, but had not admitted whether she meant to marry him.

Now it was the King's turn to dodge the question. 'Women don't always say what they really mean.'

'She must have told *you* what she really means.'

'She means' – the King paused – 'to please me.'

'Then, if it pleased you, she would leave England.'

'It would not please me.'

'Even though some would say it is your duty? Even though it would avert the crisis?'

The King gazed at him in silence. Monckton waited for an answer, as many others not in the room were waiting. No answer came.

Monckton shrugged politely. 'Then, as I have said, you must wait and see, Sir.'

'And, as I have said, I cannot let the day of my Coronation approach without making my intention plain. In any case, it seems that they will not allow me to keep silence any longer.'

'You have supporters in Parliament,' Monckton told him. 'Winston Churchill, for example, will be loyal.'

The King stood at the window, looking over the park. 'I cannot put his loyalty to so bitter a test.' He turned around. 'No, Walter, I shall send for Mr Baldwin very soon, and say what must be said.'

With that message to Baldwin, Monckton left. When Baldwin heard it, he wanted to know just what the King would have to say. 'And then, Monckton, what am I to do?'

'Go to him when he summons you, and listen to what he says.'

While the King was with Monckton, Mrs Simpson and Aunt Bessie were visited at the Fort by Lady Colefax. Mrs Simpson was by now plainly miserable, under the gathering storm. She complained that, except in her sanctuary here, she was being nagged on all sides, by people professing to be friends, to quit England, with or without telling the King first. 'They do not understand that, if I did so, the King would come after me regardless of anything. They would then get their scandal in far worse form than they are getting it now.'

From that, Lady Colefax distilled the question, had the King ever suggested marriage?

'Marriage?' Mrs Simpson repeated, raising her eyebrows in surprise. 'Of course not.'

When the King returned from Windsor, he took her into the study, opened one of the red boxes, and handed her Hardinge's letter. 'Wallis,' he said, 'I want you to read this alone. After you've read it, I think you'll agree that there is only one thing for me to do – send for Mr Baldwin.' He left her alone in the room.

On his return, she sat still staring at the letter, as shaken as he had been by it. Somewhere in her mind she had always expected it would come to this, and that same part of her mind was now telling her, begging her, to quit the country, as Hardinge wanted. It was all she could do : the alternative course would lead to tragedy.

As soon as she voiced the thought, the King dismissed it. Hardinge's letter was a 'gross impertinence', and he would not heed it.

All the same, she answered, the letter was sincerely meant, as a warning that the Government would insist he give her up.

'They can't stop me.'

'But David . . .'

'On the throne or off, I'm going to marry you.'

' "Or off" – what do you mean?'

'I shall tell Mr Baldwin that, if the country won't approve our marrying, I'm ready to go.'

'David, it is madness,' she cried. The horror of the dilemma was indeed one that might lead to madness. She was being torn as a woman in love with a married man can be torn.

'In any event,' he was saying, 'I've got to have it out with Baldwin. I am far from giving up. There are things I still can do.'

'Yes,' she agreed gratefully. She remembered the deference he commanded, the adulataion she had witnessed, the power of the golden key he held. All that could not be lightly set aside by a huddle of grey heads in Westminster. 'He is your Prime Minister,' she said. 'You are the King.'

'He has the real power, Wallis.'

'But so do you. And you have rights : the rights of a King. Stand up for them, David.'

'Yes,' he said, 'my rights – and as King, I will marry whom I wish.'

CHAPTER TEN

Before he met Baldwin again, the King wanted advice on his constitutional position. He sent for the Attorney-General, Sir Donald Somervell, to come to the Palace.

When Hardinge entered to announce Somervell's arrival, the King, in a crisp voice, told him, 'While I am speaking to the Attorney-General, put a telephone call through to Lord Beaverbrook.'

Hardinge, standing stiffly by the door, had not had a word of acknowledgment of his letter. He supposed that it was probably because of his warning that the press would not remain silent that the King wanted to consult Beaverbrook. 'Has Your Majesty anything urgent to say to Lord Beaverbrook?'

'That is for me to judge.'

There was a difficulty, Hardinge explained. Beaverbrook was at sea, on a liner to New York.

'Then put in a radio call to him. Now send in the Attorney-General.' When Somervell was seated, the King asked him, 'Sir Donald, is the King of England free to choose his own consort?'

'Two views are tenable, Sir.' Somervell had the lawyer's dry precision of voice. Which came first, the King wondered, the voice or the vocation? 'One is that the sovereign may marry anyone who is approved by the Prime Minister and the Government of the day. The other, rather less precise, is that he may marry any woman who is not generally regarded as unsuitable to be his Queen.'

'What renders a woman unsuitable?' the King asked. 'Being a commoner?'

'Not necessarily, Sir.' Boldly, he looked straight at the King. 'Being divorced.'

The King's fists tightened. Where was charity in this constitutional religion? He controlled his wrath. He needed more advice. 'Suppose,' he said, 'there were some technical obstacle, such as divorce, and suppose the Prime Minister and the Government were prepared to approve the marriage notwithstanding?'

'They *could* not approve, Sir.'

'Suppose, man, *suppose*.'

'No clergyman of the Church of England would consent to conduct the marriage.'

'A civil wedding?'

'Unconstitutional for the sovereign.'

'But again, *suppose* there were such a wedding?'

'The Archbishop of Canterbury would refuse to crown either of them.'

'What if the marriage were made *after* the Coronation?'

'Then the King' – Somervell used the name for the first time – 'would be dishonoured.'

The King nodded curtly. 'Yes, you are right.' That he had lately put the same point to Monckton did not make it any more acceptable in Somervell's mouth. Wallis had told him to stand up for his rights. What were the King's rights, if they did not include his right to marry, by any means, the woman he loved? 'Of course I have thought a great deal about honour and truth and that would go against both. But it is the sort of expedient that is suggested ... by despair.'

The telephone rang. It was Beaverbrook, just recognizable through the radio-telephone static. The King had to shout down the line, to give him a synopsis of the position created by Hardinge's letter, and to appeal to him to turn round on the New York quay and take the next ship back. Beaverbrook, appalled by the King's readiness to bellow such confidences over the air-waves, agreed to return at once.

Even Aunt Bessie was saying it now, as she knitted. Wouldn't it perhaps be better to do what everyone was telling Wallis to do, quit the country and put an end to all this confusion and misery, that was bringing no one any joy?

Wallis was simmering. 'It is out of the question. He will not let me go.'

'So you stay,' Aunt Bessie replied imperturbably, 'and then what happens?'

'He is the King. It is for him to say what will happen, in his kingdom.'

'His kingdom could reject him, Wallis. They've turned kings out of England before now, you know.'

'Because they were tyrants, or papists, or just wicked.' She picked up a copy of the *Daily Mail* and handed it to her aunt. 'Look at those faces, the sailors he was inspecting at Southampton. What do you see on those faces, Aunt Merryman? Isn't it adulation? His people love him, and his Government would not dare to do him harm.'

Stanley Baldwin arrived punctually at the Palace at six-thirty. It was to be a much less tentative interview than that first one, when they had spent an hour beating around the bushes at Fort Belvedere. By now, the imminent crisis had wonderfully concentrated both their minds.

The King came straight to the point. 'I understand, Prime Minister, that you and several members of the Cabinet have some fear lest a constitutional crisis arise over my friendship with Mrs Simpson?'

'That is true, Sir. This friendship of yours, it isn't one that the Cabinet can approve. Or the country, if I may say so.'

'Is the King not free to choose his own friends, Mr Baldwin? Does he not enjoy that right?'

'The King is different from everybody else, Sir. The position of his friends is different' – Baldwin took a breath – 'in particular that of a woman whom he wishes to marry, who will become Queen. The King is not altogether free to choose in that respect. He does not enjoy that right unfettered. It is the price he pays for the privilege of the crown. He must listen to the voice of his people. Their feelings must be taken into account.'

'So far,' the King said, 'I have heard only the voice of the Cabinet.'

Baldwin's reprimand came quickly. 'The elected representatives of the people, Sir.'

The King nodded in acknowledgment of his error. To his surprise, he found that he had relaxed. It was not all over, not nearly; yet he had now glimpsed the end of it all, and was starting to resign himself to it, almost to savour it, luxuriously. His manner to Baldwin softened into the wistful charm for which he was famous.

Baldwin was, meanwhile, saying, 'I take it upon myself to tell you, for the people, Sir, that your friendship with Mrs Simpson inflicts uneasiness and doubt upon us all.'

'I can understand,' the King told him, 'that you should wish such doubt to be resolved. So I want you to be the first to know, Mr Baldwin, as representative of the people, that I mean to marry Mrs Simpson. I have looked at it from all sides. I have made up my mind and nothing will alter it. If I must, to marry her, I mean even to abdicate.'

It was the sweet simplicity with which the King spoke, as much as the portent of his words, that staggered Baldwin. 'This is a very grave decision, Sir,' he muttered. 'I am deeply distressed.' He looked beseechingly at the King. 'This . . . is not worthy, Sir.' The King frowned, and Baldwin decided to change tack for the moment. He began to talk about the decree *nisi*, that it might not be sound, that the King's Proctor might be investigating.

The King cut him short. 'The King's Proctor may not proceed against the King.'

Baldwin heard little of it. He was wondering how to return to the dreadful subject of abdication. Eventually, he took from his pocket two letters and laid them on the desk. 'From Mackenzie King of Canada, Sir,' he explained, 'and Bruce of Australia. The throne is what holds the

Empire together, that is what they say, both of them. Sir, what you propose might break up an Empire.'

The King hardly glanced at the letters lying before him. 'If the British Empire is worth preserving,' he replied, 'it will survive without me.' He smiled, and the note of exaltation entered his voice again. 'I love Mrs Simpson, and I mean to marry her as soon as she is finally free.'

There were tears in Baldwin's eyes. 'Oh dear God, where is your duty, Sir?' he asked, stricken. 'Where is your country? At times like these . . .'

'I have one duty to Mrs Simpson, to marry her as I have sworn. That, I think, is how an English gentleman – the *first* among English gentlemen – is required to behave. Once I am married to her, I could do my other duty, as King of England, all the better.'

'You cannot marry her and stay as King.' Baldwin wrung his hands.

'Then I shall marry her and go.' The King rose. 'I have made up my mind and I shall abdicate in favour of my brother. I mean to go and acquaint my mother this evening, and my family. Please don't mention my decision except to trusted Privy Councillors until I give you permission.'

Baldwin stood. 'I can hardly bear to hear your words, Sir.'

Quietly, the King replied, 'I find it hard to say them.' He held out his hand. Baldwin took it, and they stood, looking into each other's faces.

'Well, Sir,' Baldwin said, 'whatever happens, my Mrs and I wish you happiness from the depths of our souls.'

At that, the King, too, started to weep.

The family had to be faced, immediately. From the Palace, the King went to dine with his mother and sister at Marlborough House, and told them what he had chosen to do. 'I have grown to love her more and more as the years have passed. I mean to marry her. That is all I can say, Mama.'

'You must find more to say than that.' Queen Mary told him. For months, she had been in an agony of shame for him, reading the filth in the American papers, hearing Hardinge's reports, and always dreading that it would come to this, her eldest son humiliating her more cruelly than anyone had in her life. The pain was hers alone, now. She did not have his father to turn to : the father who always had as much difficulty as she had in talking to their children, but who could be depended on to shield her from the worst embarrassments; the father who, like her, had always put his country before everything else. 'How,' she demanded, 'are you to justify yourself to your mother and your sister?'

'I love Wallis.'

'*Love?*' The Queen threw the word back at him with contempt. 'Where is your love for me? For your dead father? For your sister? For your country, David? What is this talk of "love"? This talk of "I"? Are we to think only of you? All the sacrifices that were made for this country, during those four terrible years of war, by loyal men, simple men, and now you, their *King*, cannot make a much lesser sacrifice. All the real love that was shown then by your father's subjects, and now you, his son, are chattering of what you choose to call your "love" for this – this woman, from a foreign land. David, I implore you to go away and reconsider. I implore you to do that.'

The King was shaken. It was worse even than he had feared. But he would not budge. 'I mean to marry her, Mama. It is my only happiness.'

The Queen turned to the Princess Mary. '*His* only happiness!' She faced him again. 'And the Government? The Prime Minister? Have you deigned to hear what they might say?'

'I have heard. They do not understand me, any more than you do, Mama. If I have to, I shall abdicate. I have told Mr Baldwin so.'

The Queen rose, and stood with great dignity. 'You will *desert.*'

'Resign. For someone I love more than anything else. Mama, if I might bring Wallis here for you to meet her, for the two of you to talk to each other, mightn't you perhaps come to understand?'

'I understand clearly enough already.' The Queen rested her hand on her daughter's shoulder. 'My son intends to embarrass this country ... for a woman. Contemptible in any man; in you, abominable. Of course you may not bring her to talk with me. I'm sorry it's impossible. I cannot bear for you to speak only of your happiness. After all these years of your father's example, you surely know that for *us* duty is the only happiness.'

The next day, the King told each of his brothers of the choice he intended to make. Bertie, Duke of York, next in line of succession to the throne, was so taken aback that he could not speak. The King told him, 'You can all be sure of one thing. I shall go, if go I must, quietly and with dignity.'

The Duke of Kent, the King's closest friend when they were younger, concealed his feelings from the King, but shared his rage with Baldwin. 'He is besotted with the woman,' he declared. 'One can't get a word of sense out of him.'

The Queen also confided in Baldwin. 'Well, Prime Minister,' she greeted him, with a warmth she had never shown him in calmer days, 'here's a pretty kettle of fish.'

'Oh Ma'am,' he answered, 'I don't know what to say to you.'

She had expected it, she told him, but it had arrived nevertheless as a painful blow to her pride. 'There has been no real struggle in him, no moral effort. It is all talk of self, talk of what he imagines will be his happiness. And he was so promising, until he met that woman.' She stood together with Baldwin at the window overlooking St James's Park. 'What shall we do,' she asked, 'if he persists?'

'I would not have wished to say this to you of all people, Ma'am : but if he persists, I think he cannot stay.'

'And I would not have wished to say this to you, Mr Baldwin : but if he persists, he is not fit to stay.'

Mrs Simpson knew that momentous meetings were taking place. The King did not tell her exactly what was being said – 'I must work things out my own way,' he explained – but it was not hard for her to make shrewd guesses.

She confided in her aunt. 'I can tell you, because he will have told them. David has been telling the Prime Minister and his own family that he intends to marry me.' When Aunt Bessie, discountenanced, reminded her niece of her recent denials of any such intention, Mrs Simpson bridled. 'What I denied was that the *King* had suggested marriage. Well, he has now.'

Elsewhere, among her circle of friends, she still had to sustain an evasive discretion. Nothing went unnoticed, however. Her moods, expressions, appointments, casual remarks, all were collected and studied as though they were the form lines for the Oaks. Most revealing of all were the yet more lustrous jewels she was wearing.

'I hope he doesn't give her any of the family jewels,' Duff Cooper remarked. 'Then the balloon would certainly go up in Marlborough House.'

'He may,' his wife said, 'if he really means to marry her.'

'You think he does?' Lady Colefax asked. 'She denied any knowledge of it to me the other day.'

'That may be the impression she wants to give,' Diana Cooper answered, 'in case it goes wrong for her. But it's my bet they mean to be married, secretly perhaps, after the Coronation.'

Cooper himself was shortly let in on the secret. The King, with Baldwin's permission, was consulting junior members of the Cabinet, in the hope that they might prove more sympathetic to his case (as Baldwin himself feared they might, though he did not tell the King that). Only Duff Cooper, as a friend, was. He suggested a postponement of the marriage, well beyond the six months of the decree *nisi*, until perhaps a year after the Coronation. During that time, he proposed, the King and Mrs Simpson should not meet : the King might attend a Durbar in India. Meanwhile, they could think things over.

The King saw through it, and did not like what he saw. 'You hope,' he said sharply, 'that I shall become so pleased with my position that I shall give her up.'

Cooper nodded dumbly. Or, he thought to himself, pray God you might meet someone else.

'I shall not give her up,' the King declared. 'I shall not postpone our marriage a day longer than I need. For me to be crowned and anointed, knowing that I meant to marry against the laws of the Church, would be to take the Sacrament with a lie upon my lips.'

As he left the Palace, Cooper reflected that he had never heard the King speak so piously. Indeed, since succeeding his father, he had given offence by seldom attending church. But it was different now. Everything was different now.

Monckton's appointment as go-between to Downing Street did not preclude him from keeping in close touch with the official liaison, Hardinge. It would, in fact, have been a dereliction of duty in so political a man if he had not done so. Hardinge did not mind. It assisted him, too. The King had never mentioned the letter, had maintained a cold politeness, and had even started to thaw a little, after completing his confrontations with his mother and with Baldwin.

On 17 November, the day before the King undertook a tour of the depressed areas in South Wales, Hardinge and Monckton sat with a decanter of port at their club reviewing the position. The press was still silent, but it remained to be seen what line Beaverbrook would take when he was back from his double sea voyage. 'The King thinks he will take his side,' Hardinge observed.

'Even Beaverbrook cannot keep the hounds muzzled for

ever,' Monckton answered. 'As it is, you know why Dawson and the rest are keeping quiet for the present. They don't want to embarrass the King before he makes his tour of Wales. They are sensitive enough to see that any man faced with that ordeal must be spared any other. Nor would they wish to discredit whatever effect he might achieve down there.'

The Queen saw that too, and swallowed her anger to write the King 'a line of true sympathy in the difficult position in which you are placed – I have been thinking of you all day, hoping you are making a wise decision for your future – I fear your visit to Wales will be trying in more ways than one, with this momentous action hanging over your head.'

He carried it off with his flair. He came, he saw, and he said, 'Something must be done.' The industrial depression was bitterest in the Rhondda, the Monmouth valleys, Pontypool, Blaenavon. Pits stood empty, shops were shuttered. Many thousands of families lacked work, food, clothing, and had done for years. They stood on the streets, sullen witnesses to the King of his Government's neglect and apathy. He spoke to them, hundreds of them, persuaded them to talk to him, to recognize that he felt for them. At Merthyr Tydfil, he went into the Labour Exchange, and talked to those in the long dole queue. He abandoned his itinerary to visit the derelict steel-works at Dowlais, where nine thousand men had worked, and now were sitting on the rusty, demolished plant buildings. They received him with an old Welsh hymn. He listened to it, bareheaded. Afterwards, he told them, 'You may be sure that all I can do for you I will. We certainly want better times brought to your valley.' Turning to a district official, he said, 'These works brought all these people here. Something must be done to find them work.' *The Times* praised the King's concern for the jobless. He had left them a little hope.

'But what can he mean,' Hardinge asked, 'by these promises and pronouncements of his when he has already told

the Prime Minister and his family that he wishes to renounce the throne?'

'Yes,' Monckton concurred, 'something must certainly be
done about *him*.'

'You think that he must go?'

'Very probably,' Monckton replied. 'And if so, as soon as
possible. How does he seem in himself?'

'Curiously jolly. No doubt a reaction from what he saw in
Wales.'

The Duke of York was telling his wife about the King's
warning to him that he might have to succeed to the throne.
'Oh, it was so sad. And d-dreadful.'

'She is a very clever woman,' the Duchess observed.

'But how c-could he let himself g-get into a state like
this? With all he has been g-given, and all he has to *do*.
He is obsessed, blind to all reason. If she is clever, he is
weak.'

'Look how he has treated you, Bertie,' his wife said. 'He
has not consulted you or kept you informed. David has just
used you.'

'I wish my m-mother would see her. It might be that she
c-could understand then what has happened, and help
him.'

But he knew the Queen would not see Mrs Simpson. He
himself had asked her to: she answered that the King had
had all the help he should need, the upbringing, the training, that befits an heir to the throne of England. 'His father
and I were at endless pains to give him these. If they do not
enable him to do his duty, then I cannot.' But, the Duke
had persisted, could she not talk to David as his mother?
No, she replied, they had lost the art of talking as mother
and son. In her way, she said bleakly, she had loved a naval
cadet, a boy Prince of Wales, a young officer in war, an
ambassador of England, and now her King. 'But I cannot
talk to him as a son.'

'What is to happen now, Bertie?' the Duchess asked.

The Duke told her that the King was hoping to win the support of the younger men in the Government, and that Beaverbrook might help him to find a way through.

'Ah, yes,' the Duchess said. 'False hope is another symptom of obsession.'

CHAPTER ELEVEN

The King's hopes were recharged by the *Daily Mail*. In a leader headed 'The King Edward Touch' the paper praised not only the King's care for his people, which he had manifested once again in South Wales, but especially 'the royal technique – "I am going to see for myself and act forthwith" ' – which was sharply contrasted to the Government's lethargy. 'Surely those who have recently confessed that they dared not tell the people the truth three years ago and have accomplished so little towards defence will realize the gulf between their conduct and the King's methods in Wales.'

The call for political activity was certain to win widespread support; but that, Stanley Baldwin knew, was not the only message that Esmond Harmsworth's paper was putting out. It was also promoting the formation, inside Parliament and in the country, of a King's Party. Baldwin, a political healer, did not want any division of opinion, least of all this one, which would encourage the King to go on thinking he could, somehow, get away with it.

Monckton agreed. As he told Baldwin, at Downing Street, it was a pity. Just when the King's mind was almost made up to go quietly, Harmsworth had to rekindle the notion that the country might be on his side if it came to a showdown. Now he would prevaricate again, gambling that something would turn up if he could only prolong the crisis. Monckton it was who had persistently advised the King to be patient; but now it was Monckton, overcoming the streak of sentimentality in his own soul, who most ardently wished the King would do as he had promised he would : go quietly and with dignity. Instead, he found the King more than a little mad, and more obstinate than ever in refusing to listen to anything that he did not want to hear.

The Times, at least, would have no truck with a King's

Party. 'The King's constitutional position,' it thundered in answer to the *Mail*, 'is above and apart from party politics, and those who cherish the institution of the Monarchy will always strive to keep it so.' The next day, Dawson resumed the argument, this time 'intimidating the King in code', as Beaverbrook put it, by criticizing the appointment of a new Governor-General for South Africa 'It is the position – the position of the King's deputy no less than of the King himself – that must be kept high above public reproach or ridicule, and that is incomparably more important than the individual who fills it.'

Still, only a handful of people, in the estates of power, knew how to decode these preliminaries. The dams set up by Beaverbrook and Harmsworth remained intact.

The next move came from Harmsworth in person. He invited Mrs Simpson to lunch with him at Claridge's, and there he put to her the idea that she might marry the King morganatically. He had to explain it : 'A morganatic marriage is a marriage whereby a commoner marries a King but does not share or inherit his royal rank or possessions. Nor does their issue, if any.'

'So what,' Mrs Simpson wondered, 'is in it for the commoner?'

'One assumes there is a measure of love,' Harmsworth answered drily. 'And, of course, *some* of the royal rank and possessions do inevitably rub off. A subordinate title is often arranged – the Duchess of Lancaster, it could be – and the usual regal comforts are available.'

'I'm not sure I should be talking about this, Mr Harmsworth.' She was bewildered by the idea, so English in its subtlety, but it unquestionably looked an attractive one.

'It happens quite often in other countries. It's not the same thing as becoming royal, naturally, and so in that sense is not very flattering to you. But it does have a certain cachet, and as a compromise solution would at least serve the main purpose, of keeping the King on the throne.'

The King had little taste for the proposal at first, when Wallis explained it to him. It would not be flattering to her, and in any case it was unlikely to be acceptable in England nowadays. Monckton corroborated that view. The legal precedents were extremely doubtful. 'Even if the Cabinet approved, which it will not, special legislation would be required, and the Bill,' he said, looking at Wallis, 'would not get to first base in Parliament.'

'But David,' she said, 'if there is the slightest chance that it will resolve the crisis, it is surely our duty to pursue the idea, whether it is to our taste or not.'

The King, sighing from the strain he had now been under for so long, nodded impulsively. 'Very well. Since Esmond seems to know all about it, he'd better be the one to put it up to Baldwin. I'll arrange for that right away.'

Harmsworth went to Downing Street. 'The people love him,' he told Baldwin. 'The people want him to have the woman he loves.'

Baldwin had little patience left for the King, and none at all for the emissaries of what he called the Devil's press. 'They don't even know who she is yet,' he retorted. 'In England, hardly anyone outside the royal set knows the woman exists.'

'Thanks to the forbearance of newspaper proprietors like myself.'

'You'll not forbear for ever. One day they'll know all about her. And they won't want to have anything to do with her.'

'The *Daily Mail* thinks otherwise.'

'I know the people of this country better than you and your ... better than the *Daily Mail* does. They will not want that woman for Queen.'

'That is the point of the morganatic proposal.'

'Look, Mr Harmsworth. The woman the King marries becomes Queen. A morganatic marriage is the one compromise that'll have no sale with the English. Besides, special legislation would be necessary, and the Houses of Parliament will never pass it.'

'Oh, I'm sure they would,' Harmsworth demurred. 'The

whole standard of morals is so much more broad-minded since the War.'

'Yes, you are right.' Baldwin kept Harmsworth in suspense while he lit his pipe again. 'The ideal of morality and duty and self-sacrifice certainly *has* gone down since the war. But the ideal of Kingship has gone *up*, because people want to see decency *somewhere* to make up for its lack in their own lives. The ideal of kingship has never in history stood as high as it does now. And I tell you, the English people will never accept the thing that you suggest.'

Harmsworth went back to the King, and told him that Baldwin had not ruled out the notion of a morganatic marriage.

The King decided that he would talk directly to Baldwin about it, and asked him to obtain further constitutional advice from the Attorney-General.

When Sir Donald Somervell had heard what the King had in mind, he did not mince his words of advice. 'Prime Minister, in England the wife of the King is Queen. To pass an act to make this not so would be tantamount to declaring that the King desired to marry someone unfit to be his Queen, therefore, by definition, unfit to be his wife ... and therefore, Sir ...'

Baldwin, finding to his dismay that the morganatic proposal was still on the table, also had others to consult before he saw the King again. He wanted reassurances about the Parliamentary support he would get if he resigned over the issue, as he was quite ready to do. Attlee and Sinclair at once assured him that they would refuse to form an alternative government. Churchill, known to be sympathetic to the King, was not as forthright, but conceded that he, too, would in this case support the Government.

'Thank you, gentlemen,' Baldwin answered. 'After what I said to Harmsworth, I am astonished that the King still expects me to give the proposal official consideration. Is this the sort of thing I've stood for in public life?'

At the Palace, Baldwin told the King that he had not thought the morganatic proposal one that he should put before the Cabinet.

'But of course you will do?' asked the King, who by now had become attached to the idea, since Wallis favoured it.

Baldwin took a long breath. 'Sir,' he began wearily, 'let me give you a horseback opinion. The Cabinet will not accept it. Nor would Parliament pass it.'

'Neither Cabinet nor Parliament has yet been *consulted*.' The King was as weary as his Prime Minister. 'You can *try* them, Mr Baldwin.'

Baldwin decided that his best hope lay in trying to frighten the King. 'If you persist in this proposal, Sir –'

'I do, I do,' the King interrupted hotly.

'– then not only the British Cabinet must be tried, but all the Dominion Cabinets.' He let that sink in. 'Do you wish me to do that?'

'Yes, yes. I must marry her, do you hear me? We love each other. Surely that may count with all the Cabinets in the world?'

Beaverbrook did not like Harmsworth's morganatic idea at all. Landing back in England, the day after Baldwin's interview with the King, he motored straight to the Fort. The lunch the King offered him there was strictly in accordance with Beaverbrook's latest diet, as confirmed by his own staff, who had themselves checked by radio-telephone with the chef on the Southampton-bound liner that the Lord's dietary orders had not been changed during his time at sea. Such care, Beaverbrook told the King, was representative of what had made him so popular in the country, with great and small alike. 'It is indestructible, Sir, your popularity. Particularly after what you did and said in South Wales. You comforted and inspired. Your people love you. You may confidently marry whom you choose. The Government has no right, in law or precedent, to forbid the banns. But what you must *not* do, Sir, is to propose a morganatic marriage.'

'Wallis likes the idea,' the King told him. 'It came from Esmond Harmsworth. Oh, by the way, Max, Harmsworth asked me if you were returning to England, and I didn't tell him that I had asked you to. I'd be grateful if you wouldn't let him know about that.'

'Of course I won't, Sir.' It would be something to keep in reserve, though, Beaverbrook reflected, if Harmsworth imagined that this horrible idea of his had put him one up. He asked the King 'What is Baldwin's attitude?'

'He said it would need special legislation, which would not be passed.'

Beaverbrook pounced. 'You see, Sir? With this proposal, Harmsworth has laid Your Majesty open to every sort of frustration and humiliation at the hands of your Ministers. Whereas if you just marry, you give the politicians no room to manoeuvre at all.'

'It can hardly be that simple, Max.'

'Nothing is quite that simple. So here is the course I suggest, Sir. One, you withdraw the morganatic proposal. Two, you find some friend in the Cabinet to represent your case. And three, you postpone any decision until we have measured the strength on each side.'

'But what friend can I find in the Cabinet?'

'I have in mind Sir Samuel Hoare.'

When Beaverbrook left the Fort, he went to see Monckton. 'Will you help me enlist Sam Hoare?' he asked.

Monckton hesitated. 'Very well,' he agreed. 'If this thing is to drag on, His Majesty must be well represented in the Cabinet.'

'What do you mean, drag on? I thought you were for the King?'

'I was and I am. And as such I believe he should abandon this undignified scrabbling to retain the throne. Unless he decides to give up Mrs Simpson.'

'He won't give her up,' Beaverbrook replied, 'and we must not give him up.'

Hoare was not interested in representing the King's case. 'It is a forlorn cause,' he told them. 'It is discredited.'

Beaverbrook sucked his upper lip. 'You need not say that you approve the cause. Your role could be that of watching advocate.'

'My role would be that of devil's advocate, Max, and I do not want it, thank you.'

At two o'clock that night Beaverbrook, whose day had started on the Atlantic Ocean, had just gone to sleep when the telephone by his bed woke him again. It was the King, wanting to know what Hoare had answered. When Beaverbrook told him, the King was reproachful. 'You could have let me know earlier.'

'I thought I should sleep on it all,' Beaverbrook replied.

'*I* cannot sleep at all,' the King said, aggrieved. 'I must have Wallis on any terms, Max, but best of all on her terms.'

Beaverbrook spoke warily. 'And what terms are they, Sir?'

'She still prefers the morganatic marriage to any other solution. I do appreciate the proposals you made today, and your energy in trying to advance them. But the morganatic marriage is what she wants.'

Beaverbrook grunted. He felt embarrassed that the King should again be speaking so freely to him on the telephone, apparently impervious to the caution with which Beaverbrook and everyone else was proceeding. And it was saddening to hear the King reject the advice that Beaverbrook had hurried back across the Atlantic to give him. What Mrs Simpson wanted, the King wanted, 'I must tell you, Sir, if you pursue this line, you'll lose the fight before it's begun. But it's very late, Sir, perhaps we should both sleep on it.'

'I can't, Max, but of course you must,' said the King, demonstrating his famous consideration. 'Good night. I shall trust to Wallis's instinct and preference, and go on trying for this morganatic thing.'

* * *

Baldwin, sitting at the head of the long table, was addressing the Cabinet. 'In answer to His Majesty's command that a morganatic marriage be considered, I replied that I should need, first of all, to consult you, and that the Dominion Cabinets must also be consulted. To this latter end, cables have been prepared in the Dominions Office, and despatched. Every Dominion has been invited to give its views on each of the three following courses : one, that the King should marry Mrs Simpson and that she should be recognized as Queen . . .'

Along the table there was a noise of grumbling. Baldwin held up his hand for silence. Because of his own distaste for the morganatic proposal, he was more than usually anxious that it should get a fair hearing from his colleagues. He spoke as plainly as he could. 'Two, that he should marry her and yet that she should not become Queen . . .'

A low, throaty noise again arose. Baldwin was not surprised. He had told that King that the Cabinet would not accept the woman. 'And three', he continued, 'that His Majesty should abdicate in favour of His Royal Highness the Duke of York.'

Now there was absolute silence in the Cabinet Room, the silence of despairing assent. Baldwin sighed, blinking at his colleagues, took a breath, and went on in a voice that gained in conviction. 'Our next regular Cabinet meeting is on Wednesday, December the second. Between now and then I shall receive answers from the Dominions; between now and then you must resolve in your minds, and in your hearts, what you would wish to be done in this unhappy affair. Then I shall be in a position, strengthened by your advice and that of the Governments of the Dominions, to approach our sovereign Lord, the King, and state what is the will of His Majesty's people, both here in Britain and throughout his Empire Beyond the Seas.'

During these critical days, Mrs Simpson spent most of her time at home in Cumberland Terrace, resting in bed, with

Aunt Bessie to look after her. If she went out, she was stared at, by strangers. Even to part the curtains and look out of the window was alarming now, for there would always be one or two people standing in the street, watching the house. Aunt Bessie told her she was imagining things : while the English newspapers kept silent, how could anyone know who she was, or where she lived, except those who knew anyway? 'You must not let your nerves get the better of you, Wallis. You'll make yourself ill again.' And Aunt Bessie would pour them a glass of champagne apiece from the supply that the King sent regularly. If the King could have brought it himself, it would have been much more of a tonic. All that she knew of what was going on, in the corridors of Westminster, came to her in snips and snatches when he telephoned. It was never enough, never definite; there was always some new twist in the labyrinth of English political life, and never a ray of hope without a fresh cloud of alarm. If David could have come to calm her down ... But it was impossible, he was fully occupied in negotiating, fixing, exploring, and, like her, just fretting. He was in the eye of the storm, and she did not want to add to his troubles by sharing her apprehension with him. He worried enough for her as it was. But her fears were *not* imaginary, that she knew. Even Aunt Bessie could not disregard the letters that had started to arrive, most of them anonymous, mostly hostile and some actually threatening. It was as though she were a hunted animal, besieged in a burrow, and outside the dogs were barking and scrambling to get to her. She was their quarry, a notoriety.

She remembered all those smiling faces in Jugoslavia, only a few months ago, in the clear Mediterranean sunshine. *Zivila Ljubav!* Now, in England, she had learned to distrust anyone's smile. Outside the house, an air of menace to her was mounting, out there in the fog, which swirled silently under the street-lamps day after day, so that she could not even see as far as Regent's Park.

* * *

Baldwin entered the King's study at Buckingham Palace with his briefcase. In it were the answers from the Dominions. He had agreed that the King should see them before the Cabinet meeting on 2 December.

'Very decent of you,' the King remarked, trying hard to be calm and debonair about it. 'Sit down, please, Mr Baldwin, and tell me about them.'

Baldwin sat on the other side of the desk, and carefully arranged the cables in front of him. His face gave nothing away, and everything. The King sat back and waited, fingertips pointed in an arch. It was better to hear the Prime Minister's interpretation than to seize the cables and see the worst at once. 'Savage of New Zealand,' Baldwin began, 'says that he "will not quarrel with anything the King does, nor with anything his Government do to restrain him".'

The irony brought a small smile to the King's face. 'Isn't that known as trimming?'

'Sir, it's only fair to Savage to say that, on his own admission, he had never heard of Mrs Simpson before he read the cable.'

'I see.' The King was gallantly covering the bitterness of what he knew had to come by maintaining his poise. 'Caught with his trousers down, and he's made a pretty poor effort at pulling them up. Leave me out of it, he's saying, I don't want to get in anyone's bad books. Well, Prime Minister, he who is not with me is against me.'

'Let us not exaggerate, Sir.' Baldwin's quiet voice, in contrast to the King's, was unforced. 'For Ireland, de Valera merely says that you cannot, in any case whatever, remain King of Eire.'

'That's fair enough, from his point of view. He's got his own axe to grind.'

'And now, Sir, India,' Baldwin said, picking up another of the cables in front of him. 'India is divided. The Moslems are in favour of their King-Emperor's marriage, and the Hindus against it.'

'Just something else for them to slit each other's throats

about.' Then the King leaned forward, as the import of the cable sank in, and asked in a more serious, urgent voice, 'Do the Moslems mean that they are in favour of a morganatic marriage, or of a marriage which would make Mrs Simpson Queen?'

Baldwin shook his head, not raising his eyes. 'That is unclear, Sir. As you know, Moslems hold peculiar views on the status of wives. It is quite possible that there is some confusion in their thoughts between marriage and concubinage.'

'Hardly the best time for jokes, Mr Baldwin.' There was a pause, an embarrassed avoidance of each other's eye. The King was fingering the knot of his tie. 'If the Moslems of the sub-continent of India are on my side, it makes a very great difference.'

Now Baldwin did look up, and his eyes were bleak. 'No it doesn't, Sir, it couldn't make any difference whatever.' He gathered up the last three cables and handed them across the desk to the King. 'Because Canada, and Australia, and South Africa, are all absolutely definite.'

The King took the cables, but was still examining Baldwin's face. 'For?' he asked. 'Or against?'

The Prime Minister waved a hand toward the cables the King held, and looked away.

The King began to read. The phrases leaped off the paper at him like poisoned darts. 'His Majesty could not now re-establish his prestige or command confidence as King ... widespread condemnation ... counter to the best popular conception of the Royal Family ... a great shock ... a permanent wound.' The King's face, which until now he had kept brave, sagged as he leaned back in his chair, closing his eyes with the pain of it, the shame. He wished he had gone, quietly, before this.

Once again, the ripples were spreading, as those whom Baldwin consulted heard of the stone that the Dominions cables had tossed in.

Attlee reassured Baldwin that he stood firmly behind the Government : 'While the Labour Party has no objection to an American becoming Queen, we have an immovable objection to Mrs Simpson's doing so.'

'And the morganatic idea?' Baldwin asked.

'Mere rubbish.'

'There are some sophisticated elements in London who favour it.'

'Are there?' Attlee looked scornful. 'The Labour Party's ideals are rooted in the provincial decencies, exactly as the Commonwealth's are, and not in metropolitan chic.'

Baldwin was determined to be able to tell the King truthfully that he had been given a fair hearing. 'There is a lot of sympathy for the King on the Labour benches,' he remarked, 'following his tour of South Wales.'

'Sympathy, yes. Even affection. But not indulgence, not in this affair.'

'Are you sure you speak for the Labour Party as a whole, Major Attlee?'

'For the whole Party, Prime Minister, except, I dare say, the intelligentsia, who can be safely trusted to take the silliest view on any subject.'

Beaverbrook was even briefer, when Hoare told him the reaction from the Dominions, and that Parliament would be almost unanimously behind Baldwin. 'What of Churchill?' Beaverbrook asked.

'Churchill,' Hoare answered, 'will want the King treated with kindness and respect. But he will not oppose Baldwin. Max, Baldwin hopes that when the publicity breaks out, the press will also present an undivided front.'

'I cannot speak for others any longer, Sam. Things have gone too far for that. But for myself, I have taken the King's shilling, and I am the King's man.'

CHAPTER TWELVE

What broke Mrs Simpson's determination not to add her apprehension to the King's burden was the anonymous note in her letter-box warning her that her house was to be blown up. She at once telephoned to the Palace.

The King's self-control was as complete as it had always been before physical danger. He told Wallis to remain at the house, and within a few minutes she would be called for, and taken, with her aunt, to the Fort. There she would be quite safe. She should not tell the servants at her house where she was going. He rang off, and turned to Hardinge, explaining what had happened, and asking him to escort the women.

Hardinge was sceptical. 'You don't really believe that threat was meant seriously?'

'Of course not. But she may believe it. Normally she displays an iron control of herself, but underneath it she is very nervous and sensitive.'

'Indeed.' Hardinge could not keep a sardonic edge from his voice.

The King was pleading. 'Please, Alex, take care of this for me. I'd go myself, but as you know I cannot possibly get away from all my commitments here this afternoon. So many comings and goings.'

Something like pity touched Major Hardinge. 'I understand, Sir.'

'Thank you, Alex.'

As Hardinge left, he handed the typist the notes he had been taking earlier from the King. 'In order to place my household on a footing more in concert with the spirit of our times, and out of respect for the unemployed in Wales and elsewhere, I propose to make certain domestic economies. In future, decanters of whisky will no longer be placed in visitors' bedrooms at Buckingham Palace or at

Windsor, though in certain cases whisky will still be provided in the bedrooms at Fort Belvedere. As a further economy, I propose to discontinue the tradition of distributing beer money to the outdoor servants at all of my establishments.'

Thus it was that the King and Mrs Simpson were together, at Fort Belvedere – no longer an enchanted castle, but a beleaguered fortress – when the trickle from the dam started. That it started at all was an accident, in the sense that it is accidental exactly when any dam, strained past breaking-point, will split.

Six weeks earlier the Bishop of Bradford, who had never heard of Mrs Simpson or any of the rumours, decided that the King ought to be reproached for his neglect of religious practice. He wrote an address on the matter, and had chosen to deliver it in public on Tuesday, 1 December. The Coronation ceremony, he declared, was 'a solemn Sacramental rite' and required of the King 'faith, prayer, and self-dedication'. The King would abundantly need God's grace, 'if he is to do his duty properly. We hope that he is aware of this need. Some of us wish that he gave more positive signs of such awareness.'

That night, in a thick London fog, the Crystal Palace, a great monument of the Victorian tradition, caught fire and was burned to the ground.

The London newspapers on Wednesday took no notice of the Bishop's address, but in his own northern diocese the provincial papers pricked their ears at what they found a pointed remark. 'Most people,' the *Yorkshire Post* commented glibly, 'by this time are aware that a good deal of rumour regarding the King has been published of late in the more sensational American newspapers.' Such gossip deserved to be treated with contempt; but there had also been statements in more reputable journals abroad which 'plainly have a foundation in fact. For this reason an increasing number of responsible people is led to fear lest the

King may not yet have perceived how complete in our day must be that self-dedication of which Dr Blunt spoke.'

The King had the northern papers in front of him, later that day, when Baldwin called on him after the Cabinet meeting. 'The press, Sir,' Baldwin told him, 'will break altogether tomorrow.' The King nodded sullenly. 'So,' Baldwin went on, 'we must be very clear what is now to be done. You have seen the communications from the Dominions, and so you will be aware that there is no chance of the morganatic proposal being accepted. No chance in the Empire at large. No chance here at home.'

'No chance at home?' the King questioned. 'Parliament has yet to be consulted.'

'The answer will, I am sure, be the same, Sir.'

'Parliament has not yet been given the chance to say so for itself.'

'I have put enquiries in hand. I am convinced, my colleagues in the cabinet are convinced, that neither Parliament nor the people will approve of your marrying Mrs Simpson.'

'Then,' the King insisted, 'let Parliament and people say so.'

'They will say so soon enough, Sir, if you force them to it. Our hope is that you will enable them to keep silence, and your dignity, by giving up all idea of this marriage. That is the first course now open to you, the one which I pray you will take.'

'And the other courses, Mr Prime Minister?' The King was grim.

'Secondly, you may marry and abdicate.'

'And thirdly? For there is a thirdly, is there not?'

'Thirdly, Sir, you could marry Mrs Simpson, against the advice of your Ministers, without indicating that you wish to abdicate. In which case' – Baldwin took a deep breath – 'you would be made to abdicate. If you marry Mrs Simpson, you must go.'

'It seems that in reality I am left with only one choice.'

'Yes, Sir. We all hope, so dearly we hope, please believe me, Sir, that you will stay.'

'I must marry Mrs Simpson. My whole happiness depends upon it.'

'Your happiness, Sir, could surely be found elsewhere. In serving your people, and reigning over them. In fulfilling, with the help of the great personal advantages God has given you, your responsibilities and your duty to your country.'

The King's face had set obstinately. 'Only I myself can know where my happiness lies.'

Baldwin's patient politeness broke. 'But you must know where it *should* lie.'

The King's answer came in a small, pathetic but stubborn voice. 'Wallis is the most wonderful woman in the world, and I cannot live without her.' When Baldwin did not reply, but simply put his hand over his eyes, the King went on, 'Anyway, they don't want me any more.' He picked up one of the newspapers in front of him and read from it. ' "Such reproof as no one has thought proper to address to the King for many a long day." And tomorrow, as you say, Mr Baldwin, there will be more, and worse. We must protect Mrs Simpson against this.' The King was speaking eagerly again. 'She could be very badly distressed. Beaverbrook thinks *The Times* will be the most cruel. You must forbid Dawson to publish anything derogatory of her.'

Baldwin looked up. His face was drawn. 'I cannot forbid Dawson, Sir.'

The King's voice rose sharply. 'I am instructing you to forbid him.'

Baldwin rose. He was wasting his time here. 'Your Majesty, in England, the press, like every man's speech, is free.'

The King motored back to the Fort for a late dinner with Wallis and Aunt Bessie. The look on his face told Wallis all she needed to know, but he said nothing about it until Aunt Bessie had withdrawn. Then, walking on the flagstoned terrace in the foggy night, he told her what Baldwin had said. 'So it now comes to this,' he concluded. 'Either I must give you up, or abdicate. And I don't intend to give you up.'

'David, you must not think of abdicating.' She felt a crushing sadness for him. He was so promising, poised at the outset of a brilliant reign : and for her he was going to give it up. She could still not understand it. With all his power, and immense popularity, how could his country let him go like this? If only the people, the real people who adored him, could hear his case and have their say. A new idea came to her. Why should he not broadcast to the nation, and the Empire, so that at least his ordinary subjects might know the position while they could still make their judgment felt? Look at the impact which President Roosevelt's 'fireside chats' had had in her own country. And David's father had instituted the custom of speaking to the people every Christmas on the wireless.

The King snatched at the idea. At least it was something active to be doing, instead of just sitting quietly while Baldwin and the rest made their arrangements. 'I'm going to try it,' he promised. 'But I'll have to get the Cabinet's permission, and that will take some doing.'

She squeezed his arm. Something could be worked out yet.

'Wallis, there is another development you should know about,' he told her gently. 'Tomorrow's newspapers will be full of speculation about us. They are breaking their silence. I thought I should warn you. You may find your situation even more harrowing.'

She reflected, and took the decision. 'David, I think I should leave England for the time being. I've already stayed longer than was wise.'

He did not argue. On the contrary, he seemed relieved. 'It will be hard for me to see you go,' he answered, 'but I fear it would be harder still to have you stay. You are right to go. I must handle this in my own way, alone. Where shall you go?'

'To Cannes, I think. I am sure I can stay with Herman and Katherine.'

'Will Aunt Bessie accompany you?'

'No, I think not.'

'Then I will arrange for someone to escort you.'

That same night, Beaverbrook and Monckton were at their club, discussing the next step. Beaverbrook still found it hard to forgive the King for having pursued the morganatic proposal. 'I went to the Palace today,' he told Monckton, 'as soon as I heard the outcome of the Cabinet meeting. I told the King he had placed his head on the execution block, leaving Baldwin with nothing to do but swing the axe.'

'Which he went there to practise immediately after your visit.'

'The King is his own worst enemy, Walter.'

'I wouldn't say that.'

'Leaving her aside. I told him what Dawson and the others will say tomorrow, and begged him to agree that those of us who are on his side could put the case for him as strongly as we can. He wouldn't have it. He doesn't want the responsibility of dividing the nation.'

'Nor the responsibility for what the other side would do to her,' Monckton added.

'There is now only one way he can stay. Since he will not renounce her, she must renounce him.'

Monckton was tired, and impatient of Beaverbrook's crusading spirit. 'Will you be the one to persuade her of that?' he asked.

'No. But I can arrange for someone who will.'

When the newspapers were brought to her in bed on the Thursday morning, Mrs Simpson could not forgive herself for having stayed in England so long. She should have left after Hardinge's letter to the King. Instead, she had delayed long enough to see this, headline upon headline telling her what she had brought upon David. *Grave Constitutional Crisis* – those were the three words that recurred wherever she looked. She could hardly comprehend it all. Even the most lurid stories in the American papers had shown a sort of salacious goodwill toward the pair of them. Like Mrs Simpson herself, the American journalists had never imagined that the affair could affect the constitutional position of the King. However he behaved in private, his public aura was above criticism. Now, she found herself scanning grey, cold columns of print that referred to their love as a grave constitutional crisis, which called into question the independent power of the monarchy.

Bewildered, she went to find the King in the drawing-room. As she entered, he hastily pushed aside the pile of papers that he had been reading. Her expression told him that she had already seen them. He rose, and put his arms around her.

'Wallis, you mustn't let it upset you.'

'But they are so cruel – I feel degraded and cheap.'

'I did what I could to stop them.'

'I feel so . . . exposed and unsafe. As long as I remain here they will hound me!'

'Leave it to me, Wallis.' He told her it was arranged that Lord Brownlow, his Lord-in-Waiting, would escort her to Cannes. Ladbroke would drive the car, and Inspector Evans of Scotland Yard would also go with them. 'You will need all their help in keeping off the hounds of the press.'

What neither of them knew was that Lord Brownlow was also the man selected by Beaverbrook to arrange for Mrs Simpson to renounce the King. And Brownlow would not tell them. He did tell Beaverbrook about his double assignment.

The day passed in a frenzy of preparations. Eventually, at seven o'clock, it was time for her to leave the Fort. Tearfully, she hugged Aunt Bessie. The King went with her to the car. He told her he did not know what was going to happen, but she was to wait for him, no matter how long it all took. 'I shall never give you up.'

Driving through drizzle and mist to Newhaven, she was

161

convinced that she would never see England, or the King, again.

Brownlow did his best, but nothing could change her mind now. Renouncing the King was pointless. He would not accept it, not believe it. He would immediately go to her in France. Brownlow changed tack. Should she not, in that case, stay in England? His own house, in Lincolnshire, was at her disposal. No, she said. She was determined to leave the country. If she stayed, she would be yet more bitterly accused, of having lost heart and run back to hold on to the King. 'I am sure there is only one solution : that is for me to remove myself from the King's life. That is what I am doing now.'

She telephoned the Fort at every stop on the journey through France, again urging the King to broadcast to his people and ask for their verdict. Sometimes, she was observed. The multi-national pack of pressmen were on her trail, on main roads or side roads, following the car in a long procession, hemming it in when they stopped in a town. At hotels, the photographers dozed by the score in the lobby downstairs, with a look-out posted. When Mrs Simpson escaped through a rear window, it was not for long. The Rogers' house at Cannes was already surrounded by cameras when the car arrived. The siege was maintained for weeks. French telephone operators were bribed to eavesdrop on the daily, sometimes hourly, calls to and from the King.

Baldwin's face was sour as he read through the script of what the King wanted to say on the wireless. He handed it back. 'I shall consult my colleagues, Sir.'

'Always your colleagues,' the King said, in a voice that by now was habitually manic, 'never the people.'

Baldwin repeated, firmly, 'I shall consult my colleagues, Sir, but I have no doubt what their opinion will be. For you to appeal direct to the country, over the heads of the Government, would definitely be unconstitutional.'

'You want me to go, don't you?' The King stared at him, insensate. 'Before I go, I think it is right, for her sake and mine, that I should speak to my people.'

'What I want, Sir, is what you told me you wanted : to go with dignity, not dividing the country, making things as smooth as possible for your successor. If you are allowed to make this broadcast, the press will ring with gossip, the very thing you want to avoid. You may divide opinion : you will certainly harden it. But I will call a Cabinet meeting to consider your request, Sir.'

'I would like to show the text to Winston Churchill.'

Baldwin hesitated. 'Very well, Sir, I will make no objection to that.'

When Baldwin had left the Palace, the King summoned Monckton and gave him a copy of the text. Monckton's opinion was the same as Baldwin's : 'They'll never let you do it.'

'Walter,' the King pleaded, 'all I'm asking for is that I should be allowed to marry her. She needn't be Queen, just have some befitting title. I could tell the nation all this on the wireless, and then go away somewhere – Belgium, I thought – while they, my people, come to a verdict.' Seeing Monckton shake his head dubiously, the King went on, 'Take the text to show Winston Churchill. Tell him what I propose. Try to get him to utter just a word of hope. And I would like Max Beaverbrook to see it, too.'

From the Palace, the King went to visit his mother, at Marlborough House. He found her seated at a table stacked with newspapers. 'Mama . . .' the King said as he approached her; and stopped when he saw the look on her face.

Queen Mary pointed to the table. 'You have seen all these, David?'

'Yes,' the King answered in a small voice.

'You *knew* something horrible like this was going to happen : and yet you have not been near me for ten days.'

'I did not wish to involve you in something which I must handle alone, something which deeply concerns my personal happiness.'

'Your happiness, that phrase again.'

'Well, after all, it's the only thing that matters in most people's lives.'

'You are not "most people". You are . . . yes, you still are . . . the King.'

'And the King should not wish for happiness, Mama?'

'The King's happiness must lie in the happiness of his subjects.'

'And what of love?'

'You have a mother whom you love . . . I trust . . . and who loves you. You have a sister . . . and brothers. What of them, David? Have you given a thought to their happiness?'

'I must think most of all of the happiness of the woman I love . . . I cannot live without her. All that matters is our happiness.'

'If you marry this woman and go . . . will you be happy, wandering about like the Jew in the legend, with no country to call your own? Staying here a little, there a little, but always pathetic and dishonoured. An embarrassment, a royal vagrant who is perpetually required to move on.'

'Do you not want me to be happy, Mama?'

'Yes, by doing your duty to God and to man.'

'And my duty to Wallis?'

'If she were somebody who had your interests at heart, she'd want you to do duty by the country.'

'And do I owe nothing to myself?'

'Your conscience will answer that.'

Realizing that he was rather more than a little mad, the Queen turned the conversation. 'David, whatever is to happen, it closely concerns your brothers, and particularly Bertie. I understand that you have told him nothing.'

'I told him that I was prepared to abdicate, shortly after I first told you.'

'But since then, nothing.'

'I wished to spare him distress . . . as I wished to spare you.'

'Thereby leaving him in darkness and worse distress. You must consult with Bertie. He has a right to know what is going on.' The Queen rose. 'That is all I have to say. Do your duty at least in this : consult the brother who must succeed you.'

The King approached her, saying, 'Goodnight, Mama.'

She acknowledged him with a mere tilt of the head as she left.

When the King returned to the Palace, Monckton was waiting for him. He had already shown Churchill and Beaverbrook the text the King wished to broadcast. Both were of one opinion : the Cabinet would never allow the King to appeal to the people over the heads of the Executive.

The King nodded, and offered Monckton a whisky, which was declined. Pouring one for himself, the King raised it in an ironic toast. 'To Buckingham Palace, which I have hated all my life, and which I am now going to leave. I am about to motor down to the Fort, and that is where Baldwin can find me when he wants me, from now on.'

'You'll drive down at this time of night, Sir?'

'Yes.'

'Then you will let me come with you, I hope.'

'I shall be dreary company, Walter. I should be glad of yours.'

The following morning, as the King walked with Monckton in the wintry garden, Osborn brought him a telegram on a salver. It was from Baldwin, confirming that the Cabinet would not permit the King to make his broadcast. The King stuffed it in his pocket. 'No answer, Osborn, thank you.'

They walked on, side by side. 'This morning Beaverbrook tried to get through to me,' the King said. 'I refused the call. I want you to telephone him, please, Walter, and say that I cannot speak with him any more.'

'That will go hard with him, Sir. He is your loyal friend.'

'Baldwin disapproves of him.'

'You have not scrupled to arouse Mr Baldwin's disapproval before now.'

'But now, Walter, I depend on Mr Baldwin. If I abdicate, remember, he will be very influential in arranging the financial settlements.'

On the birth of the baby who was now King, Keir Hardie had addressed the House of Commons. 'From his childhood onward this boy will be surrounded by sycophants and flatterers by the score and will be taught to believe himself as of a superior creation. A line will be drawn between him and the people he is to be called upon some day to reign over. In due course, following the precedent which has already been set, he will be sent on a tour round the world, and probably rumours of a morganatic alliance will follow (loud cries of Oh! Oh! and Order!) and the end of it all will be the country will be called upon to pay the bill.'

In the House of Commons forty-two years later, Clement Attlee rose to ask the Prime Minister 'whether any constitutional difficulties have arisen in connection with the wishes or intentions of His Majesty the King?'

Baldwin replied that no constitutional difficulty at present existed, but that to question him in detail at this stage would be inexpedient.

Churchill rose. 'Does the House have the Prime Minister's assurance that no irrevocable step will be taken before a formal statement is made to Parliament?'

Baldwin answered. 'It is of course my intention to consult the House over any difficulty that may arise. Meanwhile, however, I think it possible that there may be doubts in the minds of honourable members on one score. There have been suggestions that the King might marry in a certain quarter on special terms whereby the lady would not become Queen. Such special terms would require legislation, and I must inform the House at once that His Majesty's Government is in no circumstance prepared to introduce such legislation.'

The statement was greeted with loud, prolonged cheering.

'So I was right, as you see, Sir,' Baldwin told the King at the Fort that afternoon. 'The House would not hear of that proposal. And, as you already know, the Cabinet cannot permit Your Majesty to broadcast to the nation as you requested.'

The King straightened his tie.

'It only remains now,' Baldwin continued, 'for Your Majesty to decide : shall you abdicate to marry Mrs Simpson; or, as I still pray, will you put Mrs Simpson from you and remain with us?'

The King did not answer at once. To change his mind now, he reflected, would mean publicly renouncing the woman he had asked to marry him, a surrender that would cause the noble crown to rest upon a head forever bowed in shame. 'I will let you know presently, Mr Baldwin.'

'The decision must be made very soon, Sir. We are at the crisis.'

Churchill thought otherwise. He had seen the crowd with loyal placards outside the Palace. In the Royal Albert Hall, the previous night, he had heard a fervent singing of 'God Save the King'. He had not yet heard the carol-singers, 'Hark the herald angels sing, Mrs Simpson's pinched our King.' At the Fort, Churchill told the King, 'Although you cannot speak, Sir, others are speaking for you. The *Mail* and the *Express* you knew were on your side. So too, we now find, is the *News Chronicle*, in spite of its nonconformism. And up to a point, the *Daily Mirror* supports you.'

Osborn entered to tell the King that the Duke of York was on the telephone, asking urgently to speak to his brother.

167

'Tell him,' the King said, 'I shall let him know when to come to me.'

'If you cannot speak with him now, Your Majesty, His Royal Highness says he wishes to come here tomorrow.'

'No. Tell His Royal Highness that *I* shall let *him* know when he is to come.' The King turned back to Churchill. 'Even the *News Chronicle*?' A glint of hope was in his eyes. Monckton noticed it, and frowned.

'They love you well enough to overcome their puritan principles.' Churchill drank from his glass of cognac, and puffed at his cigar. 'Take *time*, Sir. I cannot say you will win if you stand and fight, but at least you can take time to assess the strength and number of those who support you. We must have time for the big battalions to mass. We may win, we may not. Who can say?'

'Who indeed, Winston? But, whatever happens, I am *going* to marry her.'

CHAPTER THIRTEEN

The long telephone calls between Fort Belvedere and Cannes went on every day, often twice a day. No one at the Fort could fail to know what the King and Mrs Simpson were talking about, on a crackling line : the King's raised voice could be heard all over the house. She persisted in urging him to fight for his rights. He was the King of England, he was adulated, he would find that the ordinary people were on his side. Beaverbrook had told him that, Churchill had told him that, she had always told him that ; and he himself had known it to be true until he had allowed Baldwin and his cronies to outmanoeuvre him. It was not too late. He had the support of the popular press. He had only to fight back, and the Cabinet dummies would keel over. They were bluffing.

Cheerfully, the King would tell her that it was not so simple, that he was doing all that he could, but that he must not risk splitting the country. He did not tell her that he had no taste for the fight any more. His sole idea was that he must marry her. Since it was impossible to marry her and to remain on the throne, he had no wish to encourage a King's Party aiming to keep him there. As King, he could have her only as his companion, and that was not what he wanted.

The principal victim of the King's delay was his brother Bertie, the Duke of York. For days, the Duke had been calling the Fort, asking to see the King, and every time he was told that the appointment could not be made now, perhaps later today, perhaps tomorrow. The Duke did not know what was going on. If the worst happened and he was to take over as King, it was vital, he complained, that he be given as much warning as possible, so that he and his wife could do their best to hold the fabric of monarchy together.

The King was encouraged in his vacillation by Churchill,

who was issuing a statement to the press. It would appear in the Sunday newspapers on 6 December. 'Its purpose,' he told the King, 'is to ask for time.'

'That,' the King answered, 'is just what Baldwin and the rest don't want me to have. They want it settled.'

'But you must have time, Sir.' Churchill drank from his generous balloon-glass of cognac, and nodded. 'If they refuse it to you, you should imitate your ancestor George the Third, and retire to Windsor Castle and lock yourself in, having placed the royal physicians at the entrances to forbid access to your person.'

The King smiled, too quickly. The strain was apparent in his eyes and his lips. 'Well, Winston, if this move of yours does procure a little grace, I shall be grateful.'

In his statement published the next day, Churchill pleaded 'for time and patience. The nation must realize the character of the constitutional issue. There is no question of any conflict between King and Parliament. Parliament has not been consulted in any way, nor allowed to express any opinion. The question is whether the King is to abdicate upon the advice of the Ministry of the day. No such advice has ever been tendered to a sovereign in Parlimentary times.'

Throughout the country, MPs spending the weekend in their constituencies knew that Churchill had got it wrong, and Attlee was right. The people were not on the King's side. The strong opinion was that the King could not marry Mrs Simpson and remain on the throne.

'This statement of yours to the press,' Baldwin asked Churchill, whom he had summoned to Downing Street, 'what do you hope to achieve by it?'

'Time for the King,' Churchill told him. 'And time for Parliament.'

'There is no time. One way or the other, this thing must be settled *now*, before it poisons the realm.'

'The King is not fit to make any decisions now. I had dinner with him last night – as a friend, Prime Minister – and, as a friend, I urged his staff to call in a doctor. He is utterly drained. Oh, he was quite gallant and debonair at the start of the evening, but it soon wore off, and his mental exhaustion was painful to see. It would be a most cruel and unchivalrous thing to expect a decision from him in his present state.'

The Prime Minister's secretary came in to ask, 'Will you see Mr Walter Monckton, Sir?'

'Of course,' Baldwin said.

Monckton, in a frock coat, wasted no time in delivering his message. 'The King means to go. He has sent me here this morning to tell you, Prime Minister, that he intends to abdicate as soon as the official instruments can be drawn up.'

'I was with him last night,' Churchill growled. 'He said nothing about abdicating.'

'I was with him this morning,' Monckton replied.

Churchill hurried to tell the news to Beaverbrook, whose mouth gaped in a wide grin when he heard it. 'Our cock won't fight,' he observed.

'I don't believe it,' Churchill said.

Beaverbrook cackled. 'No dice, Winston.'

Baldwin and Monckton went to see the King at the Fort. Monckton was anxious that the King might be vulnerable to a further rash of scandal: for if the King's Proctor were now to intervene in the Simpson divorce suit, and quash the decree *nisi*, the King might find that he had given up his throne and yet was unable to marry Mrs Simpson. To forestall that, Monckton, with Baldwin's support, proposed that two Bills be laid together before Parliament: one giving effect to the King's' wish to renounce the throne, and the other making Mrs Simpson's decree absolute immediately.

Baldwin warned, 'There will be those who will oppose this, on the ground that it would injure the marriage laws in general, and give wrongful privilege to the monarch in particular.'

'But,' the King asked, 'you will support the proposal, Mr Baldwin?'

'I shall support it, Sir.' Baldwin was already depressed with thinking how the King was going to feel when, as Baldwin was certain he would, he eventually saw Mrs Simpson as others saw her; but if the poor blighter couldn't even marry the woman . . . 'It seems to me a very just accommodation, all ways round,' Baldwin concluded. 'If the Cabinet rejects it, I shall resign.'

And, meanwhile, the Duke of York still waited to see his brother. 'I wish he would b-be straight with me,' he told his wife sadly. 'I have always loved him from a b-boy, and I believe that he loves me too. Why, why c-can he not trust me now?'

The Cabinet accepted Baldwin's proposal to introduce a Bill for the King's abdication, but rejected the other Bill, to hasten Mrs Simpson's divorce. The case against it was put by the most vociferous member of the Cabinet, Neville Chamberlain: such a measure, he said, would be denounced as 'an unholy bargain'. It would damage the moral authority of the Government. As for the abdication, the sooner that could be effected, the better, Chamberlain argued. It was quite untrue to say, as some were saying, that the Cabinet was 'trying to rush the King into a decision that he has no time to think over. He has been thinking it over for weeks, though he has been unwilling to face up to realities.' Now it was high time the whole business was completed. The uncertainty it created in the country was hurting the Christmas trade.

'So now,' Baldwin told Monckton wearily, 'I have my promise to keep. I told the King I would resign if this happened.'

'He will not hold you to that,' Monckton told him. 'He would not contemplate it. But he will be disappointed, and he will want more time now.'

'How long?' Baldwin sucked apprehensively at his pipe.

'Days. Perhaps weeks.'

'Weeks he cannot have. The thing must be settled before Christmas.'

'Who is to say so?'

'His own conscience.'

Monckton's sceptical look expressed what both men expected from that quarter.

The following day, Monday, 7 December, Baldwin had to answer a question in the House from Attlee. Had the Prime Minister anything to add to his previous statement on the constitutional difficulties that might arise from the wishes of His Majesty the King? The benches were packed with MPs back from their constituencies, knowing that the country was in no mood for irresolution.

Baldwin told the House that he had seen the King twice over the weekend, and had conferred with the Cabinet. 'While anxious that this matter be finally settled, I am reluctant to force a decision from somebody who is as delicately and painfully situated as is His Majesty. The monarch is at present still consulting his own conscience in an effort to reconcile his private and personal obligations, as he sees them, with his public duty and the country's good.'

While Baldwin's answer was applauded, Churchill rose. 'Once again, I must insist on an absolute assurance that the House will be consulted before any irrevocable step . . .' He hesitated, hearing an ugly murmur beginning all around him. His statement in the Sunday papers had not been well received. '. . . that the House', Churchill resumed, 'will be consulted . . .' The murmur had swollen into a loud barrage of dissent, through which he had difficulty in making his voice heard. He started again, '. . . before any irrevocable step be taken . . .' The noise against him was now a tumult of howling, booing. All around him, Churchill saw angry faces mouthing at him. He gave up, and left the Chamber, still pursued by the furious din. It was a chastening experience, and one which was thought to have 'done for him politically'.

*   *   *

'My mind is finally made up,' the King told his brother Bertie, at the Fort. 'I'm going.'

'You c-could have t-t-told me earlier.' Although he had been expecting it, the Duke found the prospect of the crown overwhelming. He just hoped he would be up to the job. David had been trained for it.

'There were complications,' the King explained. 'I didn't tell you before because I wanted to make it all tidy for you first.'

'Yes, yes, I see.' The Duke sensibly decided that there was no point in seeking a rancorous row with his elder brother about the delay. There was too much to be doing. 'I'm sorry if I seemed impatient. But David, it isn't all t-tidy for me, is it?'

'At least it's all certain. I'm going.'

'Yes. But there's a lot of dreadful ga-gaps to be st-st-stitched up. I mean, like where you're going to live after you ... afterwards. And what you're g-going to be c-called, t-t-titles and so on, we shall have to do something about all that.'

'Yes,' the King agreed, quite calm now. Forty years of deference from his brother was not easily put into reverse. 'And we shall have to do something about money too, Bertie.'

The Duke nodded. Before he could say anything, the telephone rang.

The King answered it. 'Yes, who is it? *Brownlow*? What is it, man?' Something must have happened to Wallis. 'What is it?'

Through the crackle, Brownlow told him, 'Mrs Simpson has prepared a statement, Sir, which she is going to issue to the press. As follows : "Mrs Simpson, throughout the last few weeks, has . . .".'

The King interrupted. 'No. I want to hear her read it herself. Is she there?' He muttered to his brother, 'They've put her up to something. But it won't change me. Not now.'

'Nevertheless, d-do listen, David.' Could it all be going into hazard yet again? The Duke closed his eyes, waiting.

'Yes,' the King was saying on the telephone, 'yes, Wallis, if you wrote it, you can read it. I'm listening.'

She read the statement to him. Throughout the last few weeks, it said, Mrs Simpson had at all times wished to avoid doing or saying anything which might be damaging to the King or to the Throne. Her attitude remained unaltered and, if it would resolve the crisis, she was willing to withdraw from a situation that had been rendered unpleasant and untenable. She read it and waited.

He said nothing. The first, instinctive response, hurt, anger, was succeeded by frank disbelief that Wallis was not under severe duress. But then, he began to like the idea of her making that statement. It would deflect the bitterness that the British people were feeling toward her; it would go some way toward exculpating her, and putting most of the blame on to himself, which he could bear more easily than the idea that people scorned Wallis.

'David – are you there, David?'

'Yes,' he told her, 'I'm here. You go ahead with that statement if you really want to. But it won't make the slightest difference to me, Wallis. My mind is made up.' He put the receiver down.

His brother was looking at him. 'D-David, am I mistaken, or w-was she offering you an honourable release?'

'There can be no honourable release, Bertie. If there were, I would not want it. I love this woman and I'm going to her, even if I must leave everything I have behind me.'

The statement was in the next day's newspapers, and it brought Theodore Goddard hurrying to see Monckton. 'Mrs Simpson's renunciation, Walter, it is plain and it is public. Has it got the King's approval?'

'He told her to go ahead,' Monckton answered, 'but it will make no difference.'

'But everyone is reading it, and most of them are saying that this means an end of the crisis, she has renounced him, now she will just disappear.'

'His Majesty has no intention of being renounced. If she disappears, so will he with her.'

'He does still mean to marry her?'

'Oh yes.'

'In which case,' Goddard said, 'he should know that yet another affidavit is to be served on the King's Proctor, by a private individual who says he can prove that the evidence for the Simpson divorce was obtained by fraud and collusion.'

'Can you disprove it?'

'Very probably. But I shall have to go to Cannes to consult Mrs Simpson.'

'The King won't like that.'

'Why not? I am, after all, Mrs Simpson's solicitor. I am trying to ensure that her divorce goes through. No divorce for her, no marriage for him.'

'The King will not want her harried. He will see your visiting her as just another piece of carrion for the press.'

'If he wants her free, he must permit me to go to her. He cannot have it both ways.'

'That is not a point he takes very readily.'

Monckton was right. The King forbade Goddard to visit Mrs Simpson. 'She mustn't be worried now.'

Goddard went back to Monckton, who asked, 'Do you still wish to go?'

'I hardly know what to do.'

'Try going to see the Prime Minister, Theodore. He knows about this, and he wants to see you.'

'Mr Goddard,' Baldwin began, 'the relation between a lawyer and his client is the most sacred in English law. Even the King cannot come between them. Do you consider it your duty to your client to visit her in Cannes?'

'I do.'

'Then don't ask *my* advice. Simply do your duty to your client, and disregard the King's advice.'

Goddard nodded, hesitantly, and rose. Baldwin gestured to him to sit down again. 'One more thing, Mr Goddard. The lady has, after all, issued a statement that she is ready to retreat from this most hurtful situation. That being the case, surely the simplest thing to do, and the easiest way to cope with this new affidavit, would be to withdraw her suit for divorce altogether. If, when you get to Cannes, you find her to be of that mind, what shall you do then?' Baldwin smiled cheerfully at the thought of it.

Goddard, more warily, smiled back. 'I shall obey her instructions.'

Baldwin nodded. 'I will make my official aeroplane available to you for your journey.'

'I have never been in an aeroplane, Prime Minister.'

'We are all getting quite used to being where we have never been before.'

When Goddard had left, Baldwin telephoned to Monckton. 'Will you come with me to Fort Belvedere, Walter, for one last effort? He must wrestle with himself as he has never done before, and, if he will let me, I will help him. We may even have to see the night through together. I shall pack a bag.'

Monckton called the King, to forewarn him of Baldwin's arrival, and to report that Goddard was on his way to Cannes. The King at once telephoned to Mrs Simpson. 'I don't know what Goddard is up to, but I do know that Baldwin is behind it. Don't be influenced by anything Goddard says. Better still, do not see him at all.'

It was apparent to Monckton, when they reached the Fort, that the King was utterly worn out. He looked as though he had not slept since the start of the crisis. The usual smile of welcome was on his face, but his hollow eyes stared at the intimidating sight of Baldwin's suitcase. The Prime Minister was too intent on his evangelizing mission, it seemed, to notice the signs of the King's distress. Monckton took an opportunity to murmur to the King, 'I can get rid of him if you like, Sir.'

'Don't let him stay the night,' the King whispered back. His smile grew tauter. 'But since he has been so kind as to come here, even after one thought everything had been said, I can't let him leave without some sort of a hearing.'

The fact was that Baldwin and the King were equally exhausted, like matched prizefighters. When Baldwin was weary, his hearing was not acute. Thus it was that Monckton witnessed the eeriest episode in the drama. While the King sat bolt upright in an effort to stay awake, Baldwin made a profoundly familiar speech – 'think of your mother, think of your late father . . . for the sake of the country, the Empire, for the sake of everything the Crown stands for . . . give up this marriage, stay with your people . . .'

'Mr Baldwin,' the King said tersely. 'We have been over all this ground before, many times before. My mind is quite made up to go, and, by your leave, I wish to be spared any more advice.'

To the astonishment of the King and Monckton, Baldwin started to fill his pipe again, saying, 'In that case, Sir, let me begin again from the beginning. In the first place, your departure will sorely disappoint the British nation, and may well disrupt the Empire . . .'

Monckton, realizing what had happened, had a straight-faced fit of giggles. The King, realizing it or not, kept his eyes politely open, but silently, to himself, rehearsed what he would have preferred to say to Baldwin. 'I have had enough of you, old man, in your wing-collars and baggy tweeds. Your part in my life is done. Since you are my Prime Minister, you may stay to dinner, and then, off home with you, for good. I'll not have you here any longer, snapping your chubby fingers, puffing your pipe, storing up homely little touches for your report to Parliament. In only a few days now I shall be free. In a few months, by God's grace, Wallis will be free. Both of us free, she of her banal husband, and I of this sanctimonious old man. Free . . .'

As Baldwin finished his homily, he was perplexed to see that the King's face had taken on a radiance. 'Thank you, Mr Baldwin,' the King said. 'Will you stay to dinner?'

'Gladly, Sir. But first, I would like to hear what you . . .'

'This way,' the King said, leading them to the dining-room.

Baldwin put his hand on Monckton's arm for a private

word. 'Walter, tell me, do you think I have said all I could say?'

'I think you have done even more, Prime Minister,' Monckton assured him.

The King excused himself briefly, and reappeared wearing a white kilt. Throughout dinner he was in high feather, his face boyish again, smiling and fresh-coloured, chatting brightly to his subdued guests, attentive to all their needs. At the end of the meal, he had his bagpipes brought into him.

Baldwin was still nonplussed. 'He looks so blithe,' he murmured to Monckton. 'Like a young bridegroom looking forward to his honeymoon.'

'That is exactly what he thinks he is,' Monckton replied.

Baldwin's face fell. 'My words had no effect at all?'

'None, except to remind him what he is giving up. Hence his gaiety.'

The Duke of York, seated on the other side of Monckton, was watching his brother with a fond smile. 'Look at him,' he said. 'And this is the man we are going to lose. We simply cannot let him go.'

'There is nothing, Sir,' Monckton said, 'that we can say or do to stop him.'

After two choruses of '*Ho-Ro, My Nut-Brown Maiden*', Osborn appeared, with Baldwin's coat folded over his arm. Baldwin was put out, but, with a bow to the merry piper, suffered himself to be shepherded to his car by Monckton and the Duke. 'I could not have done more than I have,' he repeated to them, looking into their eyes for corroboration.

CHAPTER FOURTEEN

It was Theodore Goddard who finally brought home to Mrs Simpson the inevitable end of the affair, and when she understood that no power or popularity could keep the King on the throne if he made her his wife, she was shaken with fear and remorse.

Her last remedy was to withdraw her petition for divorce, and she set about doing it, with Goddard to guide her. A message was sent to Baldwin : 'I have today discussed the whole position with Mrs Simpson – her own, the position of the King, the country, the Empire. Mrs Simpson tells me she was, and still is, perfectly willing to instruct me to withdraw her petition for divorce and willing to do anything to prevent the King from abdicating. I am satisfied that this is Mrs Simpson's genuine and honest desire. I read this note over to Mrs Simpson who in every way confirmed it. Signed Theodore Goddard, countersigned Brownlow.'

Mrs Simpson called the King to tell him what she had done. He listened to the statement, and then, after a long silence, replied in a voice made slow by emotion. 'Wallis, matters have already gone much further than you realize.' He called his solicitor, George Allen, to the telephone. Allen advised Mrs Simpson not to withdraw her petition. The King was in the process of abdicating, in order to marry her.

When Baldwin received Goddard's message, he sent Monckton to the Fort with it. Monckton read it to the King, and added, 'In view of this declaration, Mr Baldwin asks me to tell you that Ministers are reluctant to believe Your Majesty's resolve is irrevocable, and still venture to hope . . .'

The King held up his hand. 'They may venture to hope nothing.' He sat down and scribbled a note to Baldwin, which he asked Monckton to take back. It read: 'His Majesty has given the matter his further consideration but regrets he is unable to alter his decision.'

Monckton, who had piloted the King through the crisis, now had to see him out of it. His first task was to visit the Duke of York. Before they got down to business, he was glad to inform the Duke that the latest affidavit lodged with the King's Proctor had been withdrawn.

'Why did the man ever c-cause it to be served?' the Duke wondered.

'Who can say, Sir? I'm told he was an old man. Perhaps he wanted his King to stay in England.'

'Yes,' the Duke said sadly. 'His King . . . Anyway, the d-divorce should g-go through now, and my brother will have what he w-wants. Or thinks he wants. Well, we cannot dwell any more on all that. We have our own w-work. What's to do, Walter?'

'To begin with, Sir, certain assurances would be appreciated from you. First, will you agree that your brother may retain his royal rank after he has gone?'

The Duke answered quietly. 'I think that would be f-f-fitting.'

'Secondly, may he retain Fort Belvedere to live in, if, and when, he is allowed to come back to England?'

'If and when he is allowed to, yes, Walter, he may have the Fort.'

'Thank you, Sir,' Monckton said. 'We can now go ahead and prepare the Act and Instrument of Abdication, and also draft His Majesty's message to Parliament. All of them will have to be signed and witnessed by Your Royal Highness and your two younger brothers.'

At Fort Belvedere the next morning, Thursday, 10 December, the Duke of York carried the abdication papers across the drawing-room to the table where the King was sitting.

He bowed, placed the papers in front of his brother, retreated two paces, and waited.

The King straightened his tie, picked up his pen, and signed, EDWARD R. I. The Instrument read : 'I, Edward VIII, of Great Britain, Ireland, and the British Dominions beyond the Seas, King, Emperor of India, do hereby declare My irrevocable determination to renounce the Throne for Myself and for My descendants, and My desire that effect should be given to this Instrument of Abdication immediately.'

That afternoon, to a packed House of Commons, the Speaker read the King's message : 'After long and anxious consideration, I have determined to renounce the Throne to which I succeeded on the death of My father . . . Realizing as I do the gravity of this step, I can only hope that I shall have the understanding of My peoples in the decision I have taken . . . I will not enter now into My private feelings, but I would beg that it should be remembered that the burden which constantly rests upon the shoulders of a Sovereign is so heavy that it can only be borne in circumstances different from those in which I now find Myself. I conceive that I am not overlooking the duty that rests on Me to place in the forefront the public interest, when I declare that I am conscious that I can no longer discharge this heavy task with efficiency or with satisfaction to Myself . . . I deeply appreciate the spirit which has actuated the appeals which have been made to Me to take a different decision, and I have, before reaching My final determination, most fully pondered over them. But My mind is made up. Moreover, further delay cannot but be most injurious to the peoples whom I have tried to serve as Prince of Wales and as King and whose future happiness and prosperity are the constant wish of My heart . . .'

Baldwin rose, and delivered a speech punctuated by masterfully timed muddles with his papers. 'The tragic force of its simplicity,' Harold Nicolson declared, 'was Sophoclean and almost unbearable.'

'No more grave message has ever been received by Parliament,' Baldwin avowed, 'and no more difficult, I may say repugnant, task has ever been imposed upon a Prime Minister.' He told the whole story, with homely touches that moved his listeners. 'I am convinced that where I failed no one could have succeeded. His mind was made up, and those who know His Majesty best will know what that means.' He reminded the House that it was being watched by the whole world, and asked for a dignity equal to the King's 'in this hour of his trial'. The House should remember 'the revered and beloved figure of Queen Mary, what all this terrible time has meant to her, and think of her when we have to speak, if speak we must, during this debate.' They should all rally behind the new King now, so that the damage might be soon repaired, and 'we may take what steps we can in trying to make this country a better country for all the people in it.'

After the applause, Attlee spoke in support of the Prime Minister, and so, later, did Churchill, warning the House that 'recrimination or controversy at this time would be not only useless but harmful and wrong. What is done is done. What has been done or left undone belongs to history, and to history, as far as I am concerned, it shall be left.'

When the King heard Monckton's account of Baldwin's speech, he was aggrieved. That morning, Baldwin had enquired if there were any particular points that the King would like him to make. The King sent him a note with two points. One, expressing his confidence in the Duke of York, had been included by Baldwin in his speech. The other had not: it had asked Baldwin to say that 'the other person most intimately concerned had consistently tried to the last to dissuade the King from the decision which he had taken.'

While the King was still brooding on that omission, a more distressing message reached him. 'In the changed circumstances,' the Home Secretary wished him to know, 'I feel bound to withdraw the detectives who are guarding Mrs Simpson at Cannes.' His mouth tight with anger, the

King sent Monckton off at once to register the strongest protest. It was accepted, and the order suspended.

The Duke of York was waiting to talk to his brother about money. 'There was,' he said, 'a provisional idea in the C-Cabinet of settling twenty-five thousand pounds a year on you, on c-condition you did not return to England without m-my p-permission and that of the government of the day.'

The King's face was bleak. 'Twenty-five thousand a a year?' he repeated, in dismay.

'But,' the Duke of York went on, 'I have in m-mind something rather more ample. Mind you, the c-conditions will still be the same, David. But the financial terms I shall suggest to you t-take into account the fact that under our father's Will you hold both Ba-Balmoral and Sandringham as a life tenant. If you are prepared to cede your life tenancies to me . . .'

'I must, mustn't I, Bertie?'

The Duke nodded, and swallowed. 'Then I will undertake to p-provide you with a very substantial capital sum, in addition to an annual income much larger than the one p-provisionally proposed, and perfectly adequate to m-meet your needs as a m-m-married man.'

In Cannes, Mrs Simpson laid down the newspapers. 'So it is over,' she sighed. 'I am to marry the man I love.'

Aunt Bessie, who had just arrived to be with her niece again, grunted. 'You've sure brought him down in the world with a mighty wallop first.'

Mrs Simpson replied with a black look at her aunt. It was not going to be easy to accustom herself to the changed circumstances. 'It was his choice,' she said. 'I did offer, twice, to withdraw.'

'And did you mean it?'

'I meant it.' She shrugged. Earlier in the week, she had seriously thought about fleeing to China, until the whole thing had blown over. 'I knew that he would not allow me to withdraw. To me he has been as true as steel. They don't know in England what they are losing.' She sighed again. 'We played our cards badly. We were innocents, up against some of the most cunning men in England.' She gazed at the view of the Mediterranean. She would have several more months of gazing before her decree became absolute and she could rejoin David.

Now that he was to be a subject of the Crown, the King could avail himself of a subject's unfettered right of free speech. He threw himself into the composition of a broadcast to the nation. When he had finished it, he sent a copy in courtesy to Baldwin, and asked Churchill to lunch with him and look over the draft.

'I wish I'd been allowed to speak out before now,' he said ruefully, 'not just as the condemned man's privilege.'

'Condemned men have made memorable speeches,' Churchill replied, still running an eye over the draft. 'One small alteration, if I may, Sir.'

'Where, Winston?'

'At the very end, Sir. As it stands, your last words are "God bless you all". May I?' Churchill had his fountain-pen poised. The King nodded, and Churchill added a final phrase. He passed the draft back. The King nodded again, in acceptance of the emendation.

As Churchill left the Fort, the King took his arm and walked to the door with him. They shook hands. 'Well,' Churchill said sombrely, 'goodbye, Sir.'

'Goodbye, Winston.' The King's voice was confidential. 'A pity, you know. I did think I could get away with it.'

Sir John Reith, who was to introduce the broadcast speech, was in a quandary as to the title he should use for the man now no longer King. Monckton was sent to consult the Duke of York.

'As you know, Walter,' the Duke said thoughtfully, 'he is

to retain his royal rank. In order that he should keep the family name of Windsor, I had in m-mind for him, His Royal Highness the D-Duke of Windsor.'

'But what about tonight, Sir?' Monckton asked. 'Your brother is not yet created Duke of Windsor. Reith suggests he be introduced as Mr Edward Windsor.'

'He cannot be called His Royal Highness Mr Edward Windsor,' the Duke exclaimed, with a fine display of regal testiness. 'He was born the son of a D-Duke, so he is Lord Edward Windsor anyhow, but if he ever c-came back to this country he could stand for election to the House of Commons. How would Sir John Reith like that? No, Walter, if he is to be royal, he is still royal at this mo-moment, and he must be introduced as His Royal Highness P-Prince Edward.'

And so he was, that evening of Friday, 10 December, when, after dining at Royal Lodge with his assembled family, he went to Windsor Castle and sat in a room in the Augusta Tower, where a microphone had been connected. He spoke in a calm voice, which, as he went on, gradually gained in confidence.

'At long last I am able to say a few words of my own.

'I have never wanted to withhold anything, but until now it has been not constitutionally possible for me to speak.

'A few hours ago I discharged my last duty as King and Emperor, and now that I have been succeeded by my brother, the Duke of York, my first words must be to declare my allegiance to him. This I do with all my heart.'

In Cannes, Mrs Simpson, listening to the broadcast, was lying on a sofa, her hands covering her eyes.

'You all know the reasons which have impelled me to re-nounce the throne. But I want you to understand that in making up my mind I did not forget the country or the Empire which as Prince of Wales, and lately as King, I have for twenty-five years tried to serve. But you must be-lieve me when I tell you that I have found it impossible to carry the heavy burden of responsibility and to discharge my duties as King as I would wish to do without the help and support of the woman I love.'

Queen Mary, beside the wireless set at Royal Lodge, closed her eyes. 'To give up all this,' she said, 'for that!'

'And I want you to know that the decision I have made has been mine and mine alone. This was a thing I had to judge entirely for myself. The other person most concerned has tried up to the last to persuade me to take a different course. I have made this, the most serious decision of my life, upon a single thought of what would in the end be the best for all.'

Stanley Baldwin, looking forward now to his retirement, was waiting for the grateful compliment that he had asked the King to express. He told his niece, 'His family are all wondering what will become of him when at last he opens his eyes and sees the sort she really is.'

'This decision has been made less difficult to me by the sure knowledge that my brother, with his long training in the public affairs of this country and with his fine qualities, will be able to take my place forthwith, without interruption or injury to the life and progress of the Empire. And he has one matchless blessing, enjoyed by so many of you and not bestowed on me – a happy home with his wife and children.'

In the Embassy Club, no one could be found who had ever been a close friend of the ex-King and Mrs Simpson. It was a shame that the Duke of York did not come here. One might be quite amused in his company.

'During these hard days I have been comforted by my Mother and by my Family. The Ministers of the Crown, and in particular Mr Baldwin, the Prime Minister, have always treated me with full consideration. There has never been any constitutional difference between me and them and between me and Parliament. Bred in the constitutional tradition by my Father, I should never have allowed any such issue to arise.'

Sergeant Major Tom Boothby, by the Mess wireless,

shook his head. 'We loved him. We would have marched into Hell for him. And by God, hasn't he let us down!'

'Ever since I was Prince of Wales, and later on when I occupied the Throne, I have been treated with the greatest kindness by all classes, wherever I have lived or journeyed throughout the Empire. For that I am very grateful.'

In America, in France, and elsewhere, the story would be hailed as the Great Romance. In Britain, it was a shabby abandonment of duty, at a time when duty was pressing to be done. Well, forget him, then. His brother will prove a better man.

'I now quit altogether public affairs, and I lay down my burden. It may be some time before I return to my native land, but I shall always follow the fortunes of the British race and Empire with profound interest, and if at any time in the future I can be found of service to His Majesty in a private station I shall not fail.' Prince Edward finished his speech on a ringing note of courage. 'And now we all have a new King. I wish him, and you, his people, happiness and prosperity with all my heart. God bless you all. God Save the King.'

He returned to Royal Lodge, to bid his family farewell. The Queen and her daughter soon departed, but Prince Edward sat with his brothers until midnight. As he left, he bowed to the new King.

'It isn't possible,' the Duke of Kent cried. 'It isn't happening.'

During the drive to Portsmouth, Prince Edward talked quietly with Monckton. They remembered their days together at Oxford, and the war. He had been Prince Edward then.

Having delayed their departure, they were much later than expected by the guard of honour drawn up hours before in front of HMS *Fury*. The sailors were cold and tired. When they were called to the salute, it was an anticlimax. They were just glad to get it over at last.

By the morning, Prince Edward was in France, and on

his way to Austria, where he was to stay at Baron Eugene de Rothschild's house, Schloss Enzesfeld.

He stayed there until the end of the winter. Every day he spent a long time on the telephone to Cannes. If he could not yet enjoy her domesticity, thanking her by attending to her every small need, with eyes only for her, he could at least cultivate the dependence he would now have on being told, nagged even, by her what he should do, which friends he should favour, and which discard. 'Their selfishness and self-concentration is terrifying,' remarked one of their friends. 'One is so perpetually disappointed.'

Monckton, who remained the constant emissary to the Duke of Windsor, went to see him after a few weeks at Schloss Enzesfeld. The first subject he had to discuss was one in which the Duke was always very interested, money. The settlements agreed with his brother would bring him about a million pounds in capital, and sixty thousand a year in income. The Duke had also made additional provisions for himself.

'You know,' Monckton asked, 'that there were those in favour of pensioning you off with only twenty-five thousand a year?'

'Yes,' the Duke said, 'but Bertie wouldn't have that. He was straight with me. He undertook to make these new arrangements.'

'He is being advised that the original income proposed was enough.'

The Duke's lips tightened. 'And you are now here to tell me that's all I shall get?'

'No, Sir,' Monckton soothed him. 'I am here to reassure you, in the King's name, that you will get all he promised. But there will be a delay, while he manages those who wanted the other thing, and, with respect, Sir, you must have patience.' Monckton paused, and cleared his throat. That was the easy bit done. He hardly knew how to start explaining the rest. They strolled together along the castle terrace. Neither man was looking at the view. Monckton cleared his throat again. 'To those financial settlements, Sir, there is an absolute condition attached. You must give up any idea, for the foreseeable future, that you will be able to revisit England.'

The Duke blinked. His face was lined. 'Surely I may go to my mother for a day or two?'

'You may not go to England at all, Sir.'

'But there was talk of my being allowed to live at the Fort, after a time, anyway.'

'It will be a long time, Sir.'

'I see,' the Duke replied, not seeing at all. 'Is there anything more, Walter?'

'I hardly know how to tell you this, Sir, but the King has commanded me to tell you that you should not telephone him any more. If he wishes to speak with you, he will telephone. You will not be put through to him.'

The Duke answered in a voice of wonder, as though he had suddenly found everyone speaking a new language. 'But – I thought he enjoyed talking to me.'

'So he does, Sir, except that you have, ah, been presuming to give him advice.'

'Oh.' The Duke was still taking it in. 'I see. What he's saying is, mind your own business – such as it now is. Oh well, anything to please. But if I promised not to talk about state affairs, only about personal matters, because I do miss him so much, would he, do you think, let me ring him up again then, just occasionally?'

'Possibly, Sir.' Monckton turned to look at the view again, taking a deep breath. 'But only if you also promised not to ask, as you have been asking, Sir, for what he cannot give.'

The Duke looked up quickly. 'What's that? What is it he cannot give, Walter?'

Monckton spoke rapidly. 'His presence at your wedding.'

The Duke nodded wanly, almost past understanding

anything. How could he, one man, be expected to start living an entirely different life at his age? 'My mother, then?' he asked. 'My sister, my other brothers . . . ?'

Monckton shook his head sadly.

They resumed their walk along the terrace. The Duke was still struggling to grasp what had happened. 'It would mean so much to Wallis, if only some of my family were to be there, when she becomes one of them.'

Monckton halted, and faced the Duke. 'One of them in name, Sir. Not in rank.'

The Duke's mouth opened, in silence. His face had started to work. The outrage to his vanity was a bullet in the head. 'But,' he stammered, 'but she *has* to be Duchess of Windsor.'

'Yes indeed, Sir. Peerage Law is clear about that. It is equally clear that she does not necessarily have to be royal.'

'Not royal?' The Duke's eyes twitched at a world that could be so cruelly, persistently malign to Wallis.

'Not royal,' Monckton said. 'Her Grace the Duchess of Windsor, not Her Royal Highness. Well, after all, Sir, she was at one time very taken – you both were – with the idea of a morganatic marriage. And that, when you come down to it, is what she'll be getting.'

The Duke never accepted it. Through the years, the wedding, the visit with Wallis to Berchtesgaden for a talk with Hitler, the making of homes in France, the appeals to America and Germany for peace, he could not accept it, a hideous discourtesy done to the woman he was on the point of marrying. Several years later, when Churchill became Prime Minister, the Duke thought he saw his chance. From Portugal, he sent a cable to Downing Street, requesting that his wife's rank be made royal, otherwise he would feel unable ever to return to England.

It was June 1940, and Churchill had more pressing business than the degree of precedence to be accorded to the Duchess of Windsor. He sent two flying-boats to bring the Duke and Duchess to England. The flying-boats returned empty.